COUNTESS VERONICA

COUNTESS VERONICA

NANCY K. ROBINSON

AN
APPLE
PAPERBACK

SCHOLASTIC INC.
New York Toronto London Auckland Sydney

ISBN 0-590-44486-7

12 11 10 9 8 7 6 5 4 3 2 1   6 7 8 9/9 0/0

Printed in the U.S.A.   40

*This book is dedicated to
Alice Natalie Robinson,
Sarah Elizabeth Gilmore,
and Alexandra Rachel Sullivan*

with love . . .

Contents

COUNTESS VERONICA

Chapter 1

On a First-Name Basis

"Why do I have to wait outside?" Crystal asked Veronica. They were standing on the library steps. "I thought we were going to the library together. I thought you were going to introduce me to Miss Markham."

"I am," Veronica said. "I just have to talk to her first. Then I'll come out and get you."

Veronica was in a hurry to get up to the children's room, but she wanted to go alone. She wanted to see if she could get away with calling the librarian by her first name. She wanted to impress her new friend Crystal. Crystal was not easy to impress.

The Harding Branch of the Public Library was finally open again. Miss Markham had written a note to Veronica.

". . . thanks to your efforts and the efforts of your friends on the Save the Library Committee."

She had signed it Chloe Markham. Veronica figured this was Miss Markham's way of letting her know that it was about time she and Veronica were on a first-name basis.

Veronica secretly felt that she had always been Miss Markham's favorite reader, "even when I was a terrible little show-off and couldn't make friends — before I was a well-adjusted child."

It was the first of April. Veronica was feeling particularly well-adjusted today. She had just returned from spending ten days with her father in Santa Barbara, California, over the spring vacation.

In her bookbag she had an invitiation to Kimberly's birthday party. (Kimberly was the most popular girl in her fifth-grade class at Maxton Academy.) She also had a postcard from her mother, who was on a trip to Europe: "I am planning to spend lots of time with my little girl when I get back in May. Barbara says you've been no trouble."

Barbara was a law student her mother had hired to watch Veronica. She had hated Veronica at first, but she hadn't referred to Veronica as "the little creature" for over a month. In fact, she had even helped on the campaign to save the library.

"And what about all our suggestions?" Crystal wanted to know. "I thought we were going to help Miss Markham reorganize the children's room — you know, a Fast Book Line and all that."

"We are. We are." Veronica took a deep breath. "You see, Chillo has had a hard time for the past two years. She's been out of work ever since the library closed. She's been unemployed. It may not be good for Chillo to have too many people jumping on her all at once. In fact, I was thinking that we might invite Chillo out for a cup of tea."

"Who's Chillo?" Crystal asked, pronouncing the librarian's name the way Veronica pronounced it.

"Miss Markham," Veronica said. "We've known each other for years. We've always been extremely close."

"Chillo," Crystal said softly. "That's a funny name."

"Oh, it's not funny at all," Veronica said. "It's in books all the time. I think it's a French name. It's very romantic."

"Chillo?" Crystal asked. "How do you spell it?"

"C-H-L-O-E," Veronica said.

Crystal looked puzzled for a moment. Then she said, "Oh, now I know the name you're talking about. I never knew how to pronounce it." She looked at Veronica. "Do you really call Miss Markham by her first name?"

Veronica nodded. "But it might be better if you call her Miss Markham at first."

"Well, of course," Crystal said.

"I won't be long," Veronica promised.

There was a new sign at the bottom of the staircase that led to the children's room.

PRE-ADULT COLLECTION
HOURS: MONDAY THROUGH FRIDAY:
2 P.M. to 6 P.M.
SATURDAY: 9 A.M. to 6 P.M.

Veronica was a little disturbed that Miss Markham had put up a new sign without consulting her.

Veronica and Crystal had also decided that CHILDREN'S ROOM sounded too babyish — even insulting to fifth and sixth graders. They had been planning to suggest a sign that said BOOKS FOR THE YOUNGER SET.

"I won't mention it right away," Veronica told herself. She wanted to give Miss Markham a chance to be happy to see her. Then she would slip in a few "Chillos" and run down to get Crystal.

She hurried up the stairs.

At the top of the stairs Veronica ran into a turnstile. The strap to her bookbag was twisted around one of the metal bars. She was caught in the turnstile.

"Hey!" she said. "What's a turnstile doing here?"

She looked around. Everything was different. There were no cozy wooden chairs and tables. The room looked very modern. She blinked at the bright fluorescent lights and stared at the long white tables with word processors on them. A big sign on the wall said TIME ON THE COMPUTERS MUST BE SCHEDULED A WEEK IN ADVANCE.

There was a young man sitting at the desk, but he did not seem to notice that Veronica was trapped in the turnstile.

His face reflected the green light of a computer screen. Veronica looked around for Miss Markham, but there was no one in the library except Veronica and the young man.

Veronica struggled to free herself from the turnstile and walked over to the desk. She stared at the signs on the wall. ALL BAGS WILL BE CHECKED. FOOD AND DRINK FORBIDDEN. OVERDUE BOOK FINES MUST BE PAID IMMEDIATELY. She glanced up and saw herself on a television screen that was hanging from the ceiling.

Veronica felt like a criminal. "But I haven't done anything yet," she told herself.

"Where is Miss Markham?" Veronica asked the young man, but he didn't seem to hear her. "I've got to see Miss Markham," Veronica announced in a louder voice.

The young man did not look up from the

computer screen, but he put his finger to his lips and pointed to another sign. SILENCE, it said.

Veronica looked around. "Where are the books?" she asked. The young man pointed again without looking up.

Way in the back were revolving metal book racks.

Veronica ran past the section that said VIDEO GAMES TO HELP YOU LEARN and the Audiovisual Section with books on tape and books on film.

"Books on paper," Veronica muttered. "That's what I want. Regular books."

She passed a small shelf of reference books and came to the book racks. On the wall a sign said DEALING WITH PROBLEMS THROUGH BOOKS: THE PAINS OF GROWING UP.

There were signs on top of each rack. BOOKS ON DIVORCE. THE PROBLEMS OF THE ONLY CHILD. LEARNING DISABILITIES. DRUGS. ALCOHOL. SUICIDE . . .

Veronica ran back to the desk. For a few minutes she watched the green shadows flicker across the young man's face. Finally she said as politely as she could, "Could you please tell me where Miss Markham is? I happen to be Veronica Schmidt, Chairman of the Save the Library Committee. If it weren't for me, this library wouldn't be open again, so I have a right to know where Miss Markham is and where I can find some real books — not a bunch of phony problem books."

The young man suddenly looked up and smiled in a very strange way. "My name is Bob," he said in a nasal voice. "I am your new librarian."

Veronica stared at him.

Bob went on. "You may be interested to know that I am a trained biblio-therapist, that is, a person who helps young people such as yourself face up to their problems through books. I assure you that a great deal of thought has gone into our opening exhibit, and I am sure you will find some of the books most helpful in dealing with your own insecurities."

"I don't have any insecurities," Veronica snapped. "I never did. It so happens my parents are divorced, but they are happily divorced. I am an only child, but that is not a problem. I get loads of attention — not that I need that much. I have an excellent relationship with my baby-sitter, millions of close friends, and two pets with no emotional problems — a white poodle with pedigree papers, and a rare cat named Gulliver who is part Persian, part Siamese, part Angora, and part calico. . . ."

Bob seemed a little dazed.

"I also happen to be a big reader," Veronica went on. "I was Miss Markham's best customer. But I don't like to read problem books because I think they're depressing. Besides, as you can see, I don't have any problems."

Bob raised his eyebrows slightly.

Veronica added, "Just lucky, I guess."

"Life is not always easy at your age," Bob said.

"It's easy for me," Veronica snapped. "I happen to be extremely well-adjusted."

Bob was working again on his computer.

Veronica stood watching him. "Hey, wait a minute," Veronica said. "What did you do with the Polly Winklers?"

"Aren't you a little old for Polly Winkler mysteries?" Bob asked. "Reading escape fiction of that kind is just one way of avoiding . . ."

"Where is Miss Markham?" Veronica demanded.

Bob sighed. "I'm afraid Miss Markham is no longer with the library. She was not rehired. Her methods were considered a little old-fashioned."

Veronica could not believe what she was hearing.

Bob was watching her closely. Then he said, "This Miss Markham meant a lot to you, didn't she?"

Veronica began to back away.

Bob stood up. "Let me show you a section we call DEALING WITH PERSONAL LOSS," he began. "It actually is separate from THE DEATH OF A DEAR ONE section. It might help you come to grips with your feelings about Miss Markham."

Veronica turned and began to run. When she reached the turnstile that said EXIT ONLY, she pulled off her bookbag, tossed it under, and crawled after it. She ran down the stairs and out the front door.

Crystal ran to meet her, but Veronica didn't stop. She hurried past Crystal and down the steps.

She was halfway down the block when Crystal caught up to her.

"What's the matter, Veronica?" Crystal asked. "What happened? Why are you crying?"

Tears of anger stung her eyes, but Veronica shook her head and kept walking.

"What happened?" Crystal asked. "Wasn't the library open?"

"Oh, it's open all right," Veronica said in a shaky voice, "but Miss Markham isn't there."

"She isn't?" Crystal asked.

"No," Veronica said. "The library has fallen into enemy hands. We've got to find Miss Markham right now."

Chapter 2

Chloe

"What did you say the first name was?" the operator asked Veronica. "There are quite a number of listings for 'Markham.' "

Veronica and Crystal had stopped at a public phone booth to call information.

Veronica told the operator Miss Markham's first name.

"Chillo?" the operator asked. "I am sorry. We do not have a listing for a Chillo Markham."

"Spell it for her," Crystal whispered.

"She knows how to spell," Veronica whispered back.

She was about to hang up when the operator

said, "There is a listing at that address for a Chloe Markham. C-H-L-O-E."

"It's not pronounced 'Cloee'; it's pronounced 'Chillo,' " Veronica corrected her. She had to wait for the operator to stop laughing about something. Then she took down the number and dialed it.

There was a recording: "The number you have dialed has been disconnected at the customer's request. Have a nice day."

"Her phone's disconnected," Veronica said grimly. "Let's go."

"Where?" Crystal asked.

"To the place she used to live. We have to find out where she was last seen."

Crystal sighed and followed Veronica.

Veronica had never been inside Miss Markham's apartment, but she knew where she lived. It was on the ground floor of a small brownstone a block away from the Community Garden. Her name was still above the buzzer, so Veronica pressed it. There was no answer.

"The shades are drawn," Crystal said. "Maybe she moved away."

Veronica pushed another buzzer that said

Superintendent. A woman came to the door. Veronica told her she was looking for Miss Markham.

"Well, she's leaving town early tomorrow morning, but she might be working in her plot in the Community Garden right now. You might look for her there."

Miss Markham was wearing baggy brown corduroy pants, heavy construction boots, and a big gray sweatshirt. She seemed very happy to see Veronica and to meet Crystal. "I'm Chloe Markham," she said to Crystal. She pronounced it "Cloee," the way the operator had pronounced it. Crystal glanced at Veronica. She seemed embarrassed. Veronica was embarrassed, too.

Up until that moment she had not considered it a lie to tell Crystal she always called Miss Markham by her first name. It was so harmless and unimportant, it might be called a "half-truth" or a "small fib." Veronica was in the habit of lying, but she hadn't told a lie for four weeks. She had made a New Year's Resolution to limit herself to one lie a week, "and I'm way behind," she told

14

herself proudly. "I have four regular-size lies coming to me."

But Crystal seemed so uncomfortable, Veronica was sorry she had wasted this particular lie on her. She was even sorrier that Crystal had found out.

"Oh, Veronica, I'm so glad to see you," Miss Markham said. "I wanted to say good-bye. I have a job offer on the West Coast as an assistant librarian."

"But you can't leave!" Veronica protested. "We need you in the library here. We are going to help you get your job back. We'll have another demonstration. I'm telling everyone to stay away from the library as long as that Bob is there."

"Don't be silly, Veronica. Bob is a very dedicated young man."

She studied Veronica.

"Oh, Veronica," she said. "Don't look so sad. I need a change. I'm thirty-four years old. I've never traveled. I have no family keeping me here."

"Where is your family?" Veronica asked.

"I have no family," Miss Markham said. "My parents are both dead."

"No brothers or sisters?" Veronica was curious.

"No one at all," Miss Markham said with a smile. "I need to see something of the rest of the world. Of course, I don't know if I'll like living in Santa Barbara, but I'm excited about working in the library there."

"Did you say Santa Barbara?" Veronica nudged Crystal. "Santa Barbara, California?"

"What's wrong with Santa Barbara?" Miss Markham asked.

"Nothing," Veronica said quickly. "By the way, what time is your flight?" she asked.

"Well, I'm flying to Los Angeles at four o'clock tomorrow afternoon. Then I take the bus to Santa Barbara the next morning."

"What's the flight number?"

"Flight One, the one that continues on around the world, but why do you want to know?" Miss Markham looked puzzled.

"Don't you remember? My father lives in Santa Barbara!" Veronica was so excited, she nudged Crystal again — hard.

"Ouch!" Crystal said.

"Now that you mention it, Veronica, I do

remember that your father lives in Santa Barbara, but . . ."

"Good," Veronica said. "His name is Lorenzo Schmidt. He's thirty-eight years old. That's four years difference between the two of you, which is perfect."

"Hold on just a minute, Veronica," Miss Markham protested.

But Veronica went on, "He's extremely good-looking in a sort of Western way. He fixed up a big Victorian house, and now it's all finished. There's the most beautiful garden in the back, which would be perfect for a wedding. He has a boat, too . . . You see, he designs boats. He also owns the boatyard in Santa Barbara, so he is . . . um, quite well-off. He had this girlfriend Candy, who was just like a Barbie doll, but they broke up and he doesn't have a girlfriend right now, even though women chase him all the time. He likes to read a lot and he's very musical. I've already told him all about you."

"Veronica, what are you talking about?" Miss Markham was blushing.

"I'm going to call him right now so he can meet

you at the airport in Los Angeles and drive you to Santa Barbara."

"Please don't do that, Veronica!" Miss Markham said.

"I'll be back after supper," Veronica called over her shoulder. "I'll bring you a photo of my father, so you will be able to recognize him at the airport."

"Veronica!" Miss Markham called after her. "I absolutely forbid you to call your father."

Chapter 3

Operation Chloe to Lorenzo

"Was I too subtle?" Veronica asked Crystal when they got into the elevator. They both lived in the same building, next door to each other.

"Subtle?" Crystal asked.

"Well, I figure they will probably fall in love at first sight, so I didn't want to overdo it. You know, I don't want them to think I'm forcing them on each other. But now I'm afraid I was a little too subtle."

"The part about the garden being perfect for a wedding wasn't all that subtle," Crystal pointed out.

"Well, I was referring to a wedding in general,

not their wedding," Veronica said. "My wedding, for instance. Daddy and Chloe can have *my* wedding in their garden."

"What about the library, Veronica?" Crystal asked. "What are we going to do about the library being in enemy hands?"

But Veronica had lost interest in the library. Her dream was coming true. She sighed. " 'OPERATION CHLOE TO LORENZO.' That's what we'll call it." Veronica wrote it with an arrow on a piece of paper:

OPERATION CHLOE → LORENZO

"Now the first thing we have to do is write a letter introducing Chloe to my father. . . ."

Veronica looked at Crystal. Crystal did not seem to be listening; she seemed to be thinking about something else. Crystal's parents were not happily divorced yet; they were unhappily separated. Crystal had not seen her father for a long time.

Veronica suddenly felt very selfish, thinking only of her own happiness.

"Crystal," she said. "I just want you to know that I've already decided when they do get married, I won't live with them during the school year. I'll only live with them on vacations and during the summer." Veronica sighed. "I don't want to start a new school ever again in my whole life. It's taken me much too long to get adjusted. I don't want to leave Maxton Academy. I don't want to leave you."

Crystal shrugged, but she didn't say anything.

Veronica went on. "Besides, Elaine would miss me too much." Veronica always tried to call her mother by her first name; her mother said it made her feel younger.

Crystal was quiet for a moment. Then she said, "Your mother is away a lot, isn't she?"

Veronica looked at Crystal. It was true. Her mother liked to travel. She had to spend a certain number of weeks each year at health resorts in order to "keep young."

Veronica was very proud of her mother. She wondered what Crystal was getting at.

"Listen, Veronica," Crystal said. "I really haven't got time to help you write those letters. I have to do my homework now. I told Chris I'd watch the baseball game with him tonight."

Chris Miles lived across the hall from Veronica. When Crystal moved in, he had been very impressed with her knowledge of baseball. Veronica had no interest in baseball.

Veronica went home by herself. Barbara was in the shower, washing her hair. Veronica dialed her father's number in Santa Barbara. There was a recording. Veronica loved the sound of her father's soft Western drawl: "Hey. This is Lorenzo. Down at the boatyard. Call me there." Veronica called the boatyard.

"He'll be back in an hour, Veronica," his assistant told her. "I'll have him call you right away."

Veronica sat down at her mother's antique desk to write a letter to her father. She marked it "CONFIDENTIAL."

Dear Daddy,
This is Chloe (pronounce it "Cloee", not "Chillo") Markham, who I told you about. She comes to you with the highest recommendations. Her character is above reproach. Did I mention

that she loves children and is very good with them...?

Veronica carefully picked twenty of Miss Markham's best qualities and listed those.

Veronica put the letter into a manilla envelope. Then she took out her photo album and chose a picture of her father sailing his boat.

The telephone rang.

Veronica picked it up. There was a long distance operator on the line, but the call wasn't from Santa Barbara. It was from Paris. "Person-to-person to Elaine Schmidt."

"My mother isn't here," Veronica said.

A man with a very refined voice told the operator he would speak to the party on the line.

"Is that Veronica?" he asked.

"How do you know me?" Veronica asked.

"Your mother told me all about you. We met in Saint Moritz. This is Carleton . . . er . . . Count."

Veronica's heart skipped a beat. "Hold on just a minute," she said, and she reached for a piece of paper. "Count Carleton called," she wrote. She was not surprised. Her mother traveled abroad a lot. She was friendly with all sorts of counts, countesses, barons, and other royalty.

"Do you happen to know when your mother is due back?" the Count asked.

"Friday, the second of May," Veronica said. "Mummy will be returning on May second." She thought Mummy sounded better than Mommy.

"Superb!" the man said. "Please tell her I will be in town the following week for a chess tournament."

Veronica was curious. She could not resist asking, "Is that your job? I mean, is that how you make your living? Playing chess?"

The Count laughed. "It's one of my hobbies. I'm afraid I'm just a dull investment banker."

"That doesn't sound so dull," Veronica said politely. It sounds rich, she told herself happily.

"Are you home for the school holiday?" the Count asked.

"Oh, I don't go away to school," Veronica said. "I go to Maxton Academy, which is very exclusive, even though it is not a boarding school. I live at home."

"Oh, I see," the Count said, and Veronica wondered if she had said something wrong.

Veronica promised to give her mother the message.

Her father called back a few minutes later. He was sorry to hear that Miss Markham had not been rehired, but he told Veronica he would be delighted to pick up Veronica's favorite librarian at the airport in Los Angeles and drive her up to Santa Barbara. "It will be nice to finally get to meet her," he said. "But it's quite a long drive. Maybe we should stop along the way for dinner."

"That's a good idea," Veronica said in her most grown-up voice, but when she got off the phone, she leaped and danced around the house for ten minutes.

Veronica arrived on Miss Markham's doorstep with plans to help the librarian choose the right outfit to wear on the plane and maybe even give her some advice on her hairstyle and makeup.

Miss Markham did not wear makeup. She answered the door in a pair of loose beige trousers and a rust-colored sweater. Her soft, shiny hair was pulled back in a graceful twist on top of her head. She did not try to keep young the way Veronica's mother did, but Veronica thought she looked very beautiful in a natural way. Even so . . .

Veronica did not have time to give her any beauty advice. Miss Markham told Veronica to call her father right away and tell him it was "completely unnecessary" for him to pick her up at the airport in Los Angeles.

Veronica had to spend the time convincing Miss Markham that the real reason her father had to pick her up at the airport was because he had to get the manilla envelope right away. "It's an emergency," Veronica said.

Miss Markham took the envelope. "You want me to deliver this envelope?" she asked.

"Yes," Veronica said.

"Do you mind if I ask what's in it?" Miss Markham studied the envelope. Veronica had written "BY HAND" and "URGENT" all over it.

"Forms," Veronica said. "From my school dentist. My father has to fill them out, sign them, and mail them back by midnight tomorrow."

Veronica handed her the photograph of her father.

Miss Markham studied the photograph. She looked up at Veronica and smiled. "So I'm a messenger?"

"Yes," Veronica said.

Chapter 4

The Threat

Veronica promised herself that she would not say a word to anyone about her father *probably* marrying Miss Markham and her mother *probably* marrying a count. So she was very surprised that everyone at Maxton Academy knew by the end of the next day.

Of course she couldn't help asking Kimberly Watson how it felt to have a baby brother. "I was just wondering about the age difference between you and Baby Joseph, in case I end up in the same situation," Veronica said. "You see, if my father gets remarried and has children, I would be at least twelve years older than my new baby brother or sister."

Nor could she resist asking everyone at the table in the cafeteria if they happened to know what happened if your mother married a count. Do you inherit the title? If your stepfather is a count, does that make you a countess?

In no time at all Kimberly's best friend, Amy, had gotten both stories out of Veronica — how her mother was *probably* going to marry a count, and how her father and Miss Markham were *probably* going to get married and settle down in the big Victorian house in Santa Barbara, which would soon be full of Veronica's half-brothers and half-sisters.

"Amy is so nosy," Veronica complained to Crystal on the way home. "She pried everything out of me."

"Did you hear from your father yet?" Crystal asked.

"No," Veronica said. "He is probably too busy entertaining Miss Markham."

A week went by. A letter arrived from her father,

but there was no mention of Miss Markham. Another week went by. Veronica called her father, but she could not get him to say anything. When she asked if he had picked up Miss Markham at the airport, he said "Yes," but when she said, "Well, what happened?" he said he "really couldn't talk right now. It's not a good time, Veronica."

"And do you know what that means?" Veronica asked Crystal.

"What?" Crystal asked.

"Don't you see?" Veronica said. "He couldn't talk because Miss Markham was *sitting right there*. He couldn't talk with her *sitting right there*."

"Do you think so?" Crystal didn't seem very interested. Her eyes glazed over every time Veronica talked about OPERATION CHLOE → LORENZO. She was even less interested in whether or not Veronica should accept the title Countess when her mother married the Count.

But Veronica considered this her most pressing problem — "my only real problem." She decided to consult Chris. She had already told him about the two families she was "about to have."

On Saturday she went across the hall and knocked on Chris's door.

When he answered the door, she said, "Chris, I need your honest opinion about something very serious."

"Will it take long?" Chris asked. "I'm sort of busy."

Veronica asked Chris what he thought about her accepting the title of Countess. "I'm not sure I think it's right in a democracy," Veronica said. "It might even be against the Constitution. I guess I don't mind if people address letters to me that way. . . ."

"Do you have to decide right now?" Chris asked.

"Well, my mother is coming home in two weeks, and it only seems fair. . . ."

"Why don't I think about it and let you know," Chris said, and he closed the door.

Another week went by. Veronica was running out of things to say at school. "Of course it may not be so easy at first having two nuclear families at the same time." Veronica wasn't sure what a nuclear family was, but she liked the way it sounded. "Two nuclear families with very different life-styles . . ."

"Are you still talking about that, Veronica?" Amy asked.

Veronica was quiet.

On the day her mother was due to come home, Veronica found out from Kimberly that Amy was telling everyone that Veronica had invented the Count. "She said the Count probably doesn't even exist — just like Gulliver."

"But Gulliver is my cat," Veronica said. "Gulliver is real."

"But you're always saying that Gulliver has royal blood," Kimberly said. "You know, that Gulliver is part Persian, part Siamese, part Angora, and part something else. . . ."

"Part calico," Veronica snapped. "Gulliver has four pedigrees."

For a long time Veronica had believed that her cat was an extremely rare cat. He had a thick coat of blue-gray fur tipped with white, a dark gray velvet face, and pale golden eyes. Only recently she had learned from her father that he had found Gulliver in an alley in Buffalo, New York, one snowy evening long ago.

Veronica didn't really care. She loved Gulliver even though he was a stray, but she had never changed her story; she didn't think it would be good for Gulliver's "image."

Kimberly was watching Veronica. "Is your mother really going to marry a count?"

Veronica nodded. "They are practically engaged."

"Well I believe you," Kimberly said, "but just to keep Amy quiet, I think it would be a good idea to ask your mother for some proof when she comes home tonight. . . ."

"Proof?" Veronica asked.

"Proof," Kimberly said.

"Have you ever heard anything so ridiculous?" Veronica asked Crystal on the way home. "Imagine me asking Elaine such a thing. You know how my mother is."

"No, I don't," Crystal said.

"Yes, you do," Veronica said.

"I've never met your mother."

Veronica turned and stared at Crystal. Was it possible that her mother and her best friend had never met?

"Well, you'll have to meet her right away. You'll love each other. Let's see, on Saturday morning — that's tomorrow — she usually goes to her Self-Awareness-Through-Movement class, but when she's back, you could come over. . . ."

Crystal told Veronica she was going to the library on Saturday. "I have to find a biography for my book report."

"The library?" Veronica was shocked. "But you can't go to the library," she said. "Not until we liberate it from enemy hands. Not until we get rid of Bob. I'll lend you a biography."

Crystal shook her head. "No thank you. I've already decided to do it on Babe Ruth."

Veronica laughed. "Never heard of her," she said. "You have to do it on someone famous. I'll lend you my biography of Helen Keller. You'll love that."

Crystal didn't say anything. She just stared at Veronica.

"You can't go to the library," Veronica said. "We are boycotting the library."

Crystal said, "I don't know about that. I want to see for myself. Maybe Bob isn't so bad."

Veronica called Crystal a "traitor," and Crystal immediately said she would make plans to go to the library with Hilary, who had been Veronica's best friend before Crystal moved into her building. Then Veronica said that if Crystal went to the library with Hilary, she might never ever get to meet Veronica's mother.

"Elaine has a social calendar," Veronica told her. "It's full of appointments. She hardly ever has a moment free. Saturday might be your only chance."

Crystal shrugged. "Then I won't meet her."

Veronica and Crystal did not speak to each other the rest of the way home. They walked through the lobby of their building in silence, and, when Veronica stepped into the elevator, Crystal said coldly that she would wait.

"I just want you to know that this is your last chance to change your mind," Veronica said. "If you go to the library tomorrow, I will be forced to find a replacement for you."

"A replacement?" Crystal asked in a strange voice. "What kind of replacement?"

"I was going to ask you to be one of Chloe's bridesmaids at my father's wedding. . . . You see, I will probably have to arrange most of the details, since Chloe is an orphan and has no family. Naturally I will be her maid of honor. . . ."

To Veronica's surprise, Crystal put her hands over her ears. "Stop it, Veronica!" she screamed. "You're scaring me."

"About what?" Veronica asked.

"Talking about things that haven't happened. That might not happen at all."

"Of course they're going to happen," Veronica said in her coolest voice.

Veronica rode the elevator alone, feeling very sorry for Crystal.

"If she had a happier family life," Veronica told herself, "she would be happy for me."

36

Chapter 5

The Royal Game of Chess

Veronica went home. The cleaning woman was there vacuuming the apartment, and Barbara was getting ready to go away for the weekend. "I'm out of here as soon as your mother walks in the door!" she told Veronica.

Veronica took her small white poodle, Lady Jane Grey, out for a walk. When she got back she found her cat, Gulliver, hiding under her bed. Gulliver did not like the sound of the vacuum cleaner. She pulled him out, placed him on her lap, and covered his ears with her hands.

When the noise stopped, she gave her cat a good brushing. Then she spent the next hour curled up next to him, staring into the pale golden eyes in the dark gray velvet face.

All at once Gulliver jumped up and leaped over to the window seat to investigate some bird activity outside. Veronica suddenly felt so alone, she was frightened.

She got up and went across the hall. She knocked on Chris's door.

Chris answered the door. When he saw it was Veronica, he said, "Be a countess," and closed the door again.

"Wait a minute!" Veronica called. "It's not that. It's much more important."

When Chris opened the door again, Veronica took a deep breath. "I've been thinking about making you the god-brother of my baby brother just in case Daddy and Chloe have a boy instead of a girl first. You see, I wouldn't have any trouble understanding a baby sister, but since you've had experience being a boy, you know how boys think. You could help choose his toys. . . ."

"That's nice, Veronica," Chris said. "Thanks for letting me know." But this time Veronica had slipped past him and was on her way into the living room. "What are you doing?" she asked.

Chris and his best friend, Danny, were in the middle of a game of chess. "Oh, I love chess," Veronica said and she sat down to watch.

"Do you play?" Danny seemed pleased to see Veronica.

Veronica shook her head. "But I have to learn right away. It's an emergency. The stepfather I am about to have is a champion chess player."

"Please be quiet, Veronica," Chris said. "I have to concentrate. I'm playing the Lowenthal Sicilian Defense."

"I thought you were playing chess," Veronica said.

"We are playing chess," Danny said kindly. Danny liked Veronica, and Veronica knew it. "The Lowenthal Sicilian Defense is a variation of a chess opening."

"The Lowenthal Sicilian Defense," Veronica said brightly. She wanted to show Danny she was a fast learner. "I'll remember that."

"Well, there are many other chess openings," Danny said.

"Oh, teach me, teach me."

"Not in the middle of a game," Chris said crossly. "Look, Veronica, not everyone can learn to play chess. In olden days only kings were allowed to play chess. It's called The Royal Game."

Veronica decided this was not the time to remind Chris that she was the only one in the room with a close connection to royalty.

"Just tell me the names of the pieces," Veronica begged.

Danny pointed to each one. "That's the king, the queen, the bishop — the one that looks like a horse is the knight. . . ."

"What about the one that looks like a tower?" Veronica asked.

"That's a castle," Danny said.

Chris was glaring at Danny. "It's better to say 'rook,' " he said.

"I can guess the little ones in front," Veronica said. "Those are the babies."

"The what?" Chris asked.

"Well, the children," Veronica said.

"Those pieces happen to be the pawns," Chris said. "The foot soldiers. This is not a cute little family game. This is a game of war. You've got to have the right kind of mind for this game, Veronica. It's for people who are good at strategy. It might be a waste of time to try to teach you."

Veronica was hurt. "What makes you think I'm not good at strategy?" she asked.

"Maybe she is,". Danny said quietly.

Veronica glanced at Danny. She knew she had an ally. "Besides, what do you mean by strategy, anyway?" she asked Chris.

Chris sighed. "Everyone knows what strategy is, Veronica. Thinking ahead. Anticipating the other person's next move. Trying to force the other person to do what you want him to do."

"That doesn't sound very nice," Veronica said. But she had a feeling Chris was right. She was not very good at strategy. She was always thinking ahead; she had no trouble doing that, "but sometimes I think wrong," she told herself.

For instance, when Crystal told her she was going to the library, Veronica should not have called her a "traitor." That was a mistake. She should have said, in her most gentle and sympathetic voice, "I know you're having personal problems and that's the only reason you're stabbing me in the back like this."

Veronica sat staring at the chessboard, daydreaming. The black queen was her mother; the white queen was Chloe. When her mother and father were both happily remarried, they would probably become friends again. Veronica could picture a big Fourth of July picnic with her mother and father and their new families laughing and joking together. The Count would have his first taste of fried chicken. Naturally, Crystal would be there. . . .

"Stop tapping your foot, Veronica," Chris said. "I can't think."

Veronica held still. She watched as Chris moved his knight one square ahead and one to the diagonal. Then he wrote something down on a pad.

"What are you writing?" she asked.

"We're recording each move," Danny explained. "So that we can study the game and figure out where we made our mistakes."

"Let me do that," Veronica said.

"You can't," Chris said. "It's in a kind of shorthand. It takes a long time to learn the code."

"Oh, please, just show me," Veronica said. "I'll be your recording secretary. I'll be absolutely quiet, and it will give you more time to think."

Veronica felt they were already wasting too much time thinking before each move. Veronica knew a little about war herself and figured it was usually a good idea to move fast and surprise the enemy.

"It might save us some time if Veronica was our recording secretary," Danny said.

Chris looked undecided. Finally he said, "Look, the notation system is in the back of a book called *The Chess Handbook*. Get the book, study it, and when you're ready, we'll give you a test."

"And if I pass the test, you'll teach me to play chess?" she asked.

"No," Chris said. "We'll let you be our recording secretary."

Veronica decided it would be good strategy to agree to this. Danny wrote down the name of the book on a piece of paper. Then she saw him write down the names of two other books: *Beginner's Chess* and *Chess Problems*. "That's how I learned to play chess — from those books."

Chris glared at Danny.

"They're in the library," Danny said to Veronica. "You can get them tomorrow."

Veronica took the paper. "I . . . um . . . might not get to the library tomorrow," she said sadly.

"Well, on Monday, then," Danny said.

After another hour of sitting still and watching, Veronica got extremely restless. Chris and Danny were taking longer and longer to make each move. Nothing seemed to be happening. Finally she couldn't bear it any longer; she went home.

That evening a long distance call came in from Rome. It was the Count calling to find out if her mother was back.

"Not yet," Veronica told him. "Mummy won't be back until later, but . . . um . . . she called last night. She said she wanted me to invite you to dinner next week when you are in town."

Veronica had a feeling she should have waited and checked with her mother first, but the Count said, "How delightful, but I'm afraid the chess tournament will interfere. It's very hard to know how long a chess match will go on."

"Oh, I *know*," Veronica said with such passion the Count said, "Do you follow chess?"

"I love chess," Veronica said.

The Count laughed. "Do you play well?"

"I have quite a lot to learn about the game," Veronica said modestly.

"Don't we all." The Count was obviously impressed.

Veronica had a feeling she had said the right thing. She tried to think of something else to say — something intelligent. "I . . . um . . . was just looking at the Lowenthal Sicilian Defense," she said.

There was a dead silence. Veronica was afraid she had said something wrong.

"Did you say 'the Lowenthal Sicilian Defense'?" The Count's voice was almost a whisper. *"The Lowenthal Sicilian Defense?"*

Veronica didn't have a chance to answer. Suddenly the Count said abruptly, "What evening did your mother have in mind?"

"Next Friday," Veronica said. "At seven o'clock."

"Splendid! The chess tournament will be over by then. Tell your mother I am looking forward to the evening with pleasure."

Chapter 6

Elaine

Veronica spent the next two hours calling everyone in her class to find out if they "just happened to know the proper way to address a count who came to your home for dinner."

Most of the kids did not seem to be interested in the problem and thought "Hello, Count" would be fine, but Kimberly was excited. "My mother has a book about that," she told Veronica. "I'll look it up for you."

Veronica did not call Crystal. Crystal did not deserve to hear about it.

* * *

Veronica's mother returned home from Europe that night. She was terribly pleased to see Veronica quietly doing her homework and wearing the blue plaid robe she had sent from Scotland. She told Barbara she was free to leave. She wanted to have a cozy weekend with "her little girl." Barbara went to get her overnight bag.

Veronica thought her mother looked stunning. Her dark shiny hair had been cut very short just like a young boy's. A large bang swept across her forehead. It made her eyes look enormous, and her high cheekbones stuck out even more. Her long gold earrings made her neck look very graceful and delicate. She was extremely thin, and her cream-colored knit dress hung loosely from her shoulders.

"She looks just like a model," Veronica thought, "but much more beautiful."

Elaine Schmidt was glancing through the mail and the telephone messages on her desk.

Veronica held her breath and waited for her mother to come to her messages. She had worded them very carefully: COUNT CARLETON CALLED. WILL BE IN TOWN NEXT WEEK.

C. CARLETON CALLED AGAIN. SAID HE WOULD BE COMING TO DINNER NEXT FRIDAY. THE 9TH OF MAY.

"I wonder what my lawyer wants," Veronica heard her mother say.

"He said it was important," Barbara called. She was on her way out the door. "He said you could call him at home."

Veronica tried to be patient and concentrate on her homework. Her mother was talking to her lawyer on the phone.

"But, Malcolm, I don't understand," she heard her mother say. Veronica turned to look at her mother.

Her mother had become deathly pale. "Are you talking about Lorenzo?" she asked and she collapsed into the desk chair.

Veronica suddenly felt cold. Something had happened to her father.

As if in a dream, she heard her mother saying, "Is that right? Is that right?" in a kind of dull voice, over and over. Finally she said, "Well, thank you for calling, Malcolm. Yes, it does come as quite a shock." She hung up and turned to face

Veronica. "Veronica," she said. "Your father . . ."

But she couldn't go on. She burst into harsh sobs and buried her face in her hands.

Veronica had never seen her mother cry. Her mother was the most controlled person she had ever met. She ran over to her. "Tell me. Tell me. What happened to Daddy?" She felt like shaking her mother's thin shoulders.

Elaine Schmidt lifted her head and stared at her daughter with hollow eyes. She seemed to have aged in a matter of minutes. She studied Veronica in silence.

Suddenly her eyes blazed. She pounded her fist on the antique desk. "How could he do this to me?" she shrieked. "How dare he beat me to it?"

Veronica was sure her mother was talking about the grave. Now that her father was dead, her mother suddenly realized how much she loved him — so much, she wanted to die, too.

"Mama," Veronica whispered. She put her arms around her mother. "Please don't say that. I need you." Her heart was breaking, but she wanted to be strong — for her mother's sake.

Her mother was crying again like a small child.

Veronica patted her head.

"Can you imagine?" Elaine sniffed. "Getting married in city hall? In a gray suit?"

"No," Veronica said. Then she said, "Who?"

But Elaine was sobbing more violently again.

"Who got married in city hall in a gray suit?" Veronica asked.

"Your father," her mother said. "He got married this morning."

"Got married?" Veronica asked. "Without me?" She stared at her mother. "Did he marry Miss Markham?"

"I haven't the faintest idea," her mother said.

Fifteen minutes later her father called, but Veronica refused to talk to him. "Tell him I'm asleep," she whispered to her mother.

She heard her mother say in a bright voice, "Well, I heard the good news. Congratulations, Lorenzo. I'll have Veronica call you tomorrow."

Chapter 7

Setting the Stage

Veronica did not call her father. And when he called the next morning, she refused to talk to him. She wrote him a letter instead:

Dear Daddy

She crossed out "Daddy" and wrote:

Dear ~~Daddy~~ Lorenzo:
I will not be coming to Santa Barbara this summer.

*I have other plans. Good luck
with your new marriage.
        Yours truly,
        Veronica Schmidt*

When she went to take Lady Jane Grey out for a walk, she mailed the letter.

Her mother spent Saturday morning in bed. She said she didn't feel like going to her Self-Awareness-Through-Movement class. "Besides, what's the use?" she asked. Veronica had never heard her mother talk that way before.

Veronica brought her mother a tray with tea and toast. She even put a small vase of flowers on the tray.

Elaine Schmidt stared vacantly at the tray. Her face was white and puffy. Her eyes were swollen, and her beautiful full mouth had wilted. Her lips were set in a tight line with tiny wrinkles around them. She looked so alone in her misery, Veronica asked if she would like company. To Veronica's surprise, her mother nodded.

Veronica sat down on the striped satin chair in

the corner. She knew that she had a right to be furious with her father for getting married behind her back, but she was a little surprised that her mother was taking the news so hard.

"Did you think that you and Daddy might get back together some day?" Veronica asked shyly.

"Of course not," her mother said. "But, then again, I never thought he'd find someone else."

It suddenly dawned on Veronica that the whole thing was her fault. She listened in horror as her mother went on. "Oh, Veronica!" her mother said. "I'm all washed up. I'm just an old bag that no one wants."

"No, you're not!" Veronica said. "What about . . . um . . . the Count?"

"Who?" her mother asked in a dull voice.

"The Count," Veronica said. "Carleton."

"Oh, Carleton," her mother said with a trace of a smile. "He called again after you were in bed. Did he really invite himself to dinner?"

"Oh, yes," Veronica said. "It would have been rude not to ask him."

"Well, I'm afraid we'll just have to cancel it," her mother said. "Carleton seems to be used to the finer things in life. It would be too much work — too much of a production."

"I'll help you plan the menu," Veronica said. "We could have champagne and caviar first. . . ."

Her mother shook her head. "Carleton's a health food gourmet. He's very fussy about what he eats. . . ."

"Well, then we could have carrot juice and raw vegetables with that cucumber yogurt dip. . . ." Veronica suggested.

"Then maybe a fish done very simply with braised celery. . . ." Her mother seemed to be perking up. "Of course, we couldn't possibly go through with it unless we had . . ." Her voice trailed off.

"Unless we had what?" Veronica asked.

" . . . unless we had a maid to serve."

Veronica was very excited. She had always wanted a maid. Kimberly had a maid and a cook.

Her mother went on, "And the living room looks so awful."

Veronica was surprised to hear her mother talk that way. Their living room was large — light and airy and beautifully decorated. It had been photographed for *Gracious Living* magazine, but the story had never appeared.

"It seems so cluttered with all those bookshelves," her mother said.

"You can put them in my room," Veronica volunteered.

"I suppose we could move things around a little," her mother admitted, "and we might get that Oriental rug I've always wanted, but only if they can deliver it right away."

She looked at Veronica. Veronica was pleased to see that a little color had come back into her mother's cheeks, and her eyes were brighter. "I'm being ridiculous, Veronica," she said, "but it might be fun — almost like building a stage set for a play."

Veronica knew all about the theater. She'd been the star in a school play. "Well, then, let's have him for dinner," she said. "We have a week to rehearse."

"It would be something we could do together," her mother sighed, "and it would keep my mind off . . ." Suddenly her voice faded, and the light went out of her eyes. She stared out the window.

"What's he like?" Veronica asked quickly.

"Who?" her mother asked in a faraway voice. "Oh, you mean Carleton?" She sighed. "Carleton is very attractive. He's an excellent dancer and a delightful dinner companion. He travels a lot, enjoys mixing business and pleasure. We met at the von Kronbergs' ski chalet in Saint Moritz. He was quite attentive. He's never been married, so I was quite taken aback when he proposed to me. . . ."

"He proposed to you?" Veronica was amazed. "What did you say?"

Her mother smiled. "I told him I didn't know him well enough to say anything."

"Did he really propose?" Veronica asked.

"Yes, but that was before he found out . . ." Her mother stopped.

"Found out what?" Veronica asked.

Her mother gasped. "Darling, I just remembered. There's another problem. Carleton can't come for dinner here. He told me he's horribly allergic to cats."

"Is that what he found out?" Veronica was confused. "That we had a cat? Is that why he took back the proposal?"

Her mother shook her head. "He doesn't know we have a cat."

"Then what did he find out?"

Suddenly Veronica was exhausted. Her mother hardly talked about her private life. Veronica wasn't sure she wanted to hear any more. She hoped she wasn't about to hear about a deep dark terrible secret in her mother's past.

"Darling," her mother went on, "I'm afraid Carleton is not particularly fond of children. I began to suspect something when I heard him describing his sister's children as 'monsters' and 'slightly less than human.' His stories were all very witty, but then I realized he might have a phobia. . . ."

"What's that?" Veronica asked.

"An intense fear of children. . . ."

Veronica shivered. She was sitting on the edge of the chair. It was all so dramatic.

"So he took back the proposal when he found out you had me, right?" Veronica asked.

"He never brought it up again." Her mother looked at Veronica. "Maybe I shouldn't have said anything."

"I don't mind the least bit," Veronica said. It was true. Veronica enjoyed a challenge, and she was convinced she could help the Count get over his fear of children. It would be like curing a disease.

"Maybe he just isn't used to them," Veronica suggested. "And I'm ten going on eleven. I'm not exactly a child."

"Well, you know it's strange," her mother said slowly. "When he called last night, he said he was very anxious to meet you. He said you sounded like a most unusual child. 'Extraordinary' was the word he used."

Veronica felt a little nervous. "Does he know I'm also extremely well-adjusted?"

Her mother smiled. Her lips had bloomed again, just like a flower. "He'll be able to see that next Friday," she said.

"You mean he *is* coming for dinner?"

Her mother nodded. "I just wish I knew what to do about Gulliver."

Veronica said promptly. "We'll bring him to Chris's apartment on Friday morning, vacuum up all the cat hairs, and he can wait offstage until the curtain falls."

Her mother laughed. Elaine Schmidt had a clear, musical laugh. "Well, nothing may come of it. We won't get our hopes up. We'll treat it as if it's just an evening at the theater."

"It may be a flop," Veronica said cheerfully.

"That's show business," her mother said. "Now, I've got to get dressed and do some shopping. I thought I'd start with the lovely hand-carved Mexican chess set I saw at the antique store at the corner. Then I'll look at that rug. . . ."

"We're getting a chess set?" Veronica couldn't believe her ears.

"Wait until you see it, Veronica. A table with an inlaid chessboard — pink and beige onyx squares, if I remember correctly. We'll decorate around that."

"Can I invite Chris over when it arrives?" Veronica asked. "Danny, too?"

"Of course," her mother said. "I just hope it's still there. I had my eye on it months ago. I knew

I finally had a perfect excuse to buy it when Carleton said he was looking forward to having a friendly game of chess with you."

"He wants to play chess with me?" Veronica asked.

"Now don't be modest," her mother said. "Carleton was very impressed with your 'profound knowledge of the game' — that's what he called it. Isn't that marvelous? Just think. I didn't even know you played chess."

Chapter 8

Dealing with the Enemy

Veronica turned and looked at the china clock on her mother's bureau. Her mother went to get dressed.

It was noon on Saturday. There were six days between now and noon Friday, plus an extra seven hours before the Count would arrive for dinner. Veronica took a pencil and a piece of paper from the drawer of the desk and began to calculate.

Six times twenty-four hours a day equals 144 hours. Plus seven equals a total of 151 hours to become an expert at chess. Not bad, she thought.

However, she would have to take off two hours

to wash her hair and get dressed before he came. Minus two equals 149 hours.

Then Veronica remembered that she had school all week and a habit of sleeping at night. She started subtracting hours and finally gave up. She looked at the clock again, took another piece of paper, and started over.

saturday afternoon: Research chess
saturday evening: Learn to play
Sunday: Practice chess games
monday to Friday afternoons:
        Develop profound
          knowledge of the game

"Let me see, that's five days from Monday to Friday times three hours a day. . . ." Veronica changed it to two hours a day. She was sure the expensive new chess set would speed things up.

Veronica multiplied again. Total: ten hours.

Veronica felt better. It was more realistic. Ten hours should be more than enough time to develop a profound knowledge of the game.

Besides, it was an awfully long time to hold still.

Veronica decided that as soon as she learned the game, she would save time by not thinking about each move. She'd use her Fast Attack Theory. It was probably better strategy.

"Do you have any plans for this afternoon?" Her mother appeared in a pale peach-colored linen suit.

Veronica looked at her schedule. Saturday afternoon: Research chess.

Suddenly she realized she had no choice. There was only one logical place to start.

"I have to go to the library," she said bravely.

"Oh, darling," her mother said. "It's such a nice day. Please try to get a little fresh air."

Veronica got plenty of fresh air that afternoon. For nearly three hours she hid behind a tree across the street from the library, waiting for Crystal and Hilary to come out. She wanted to avoid them if she could. She didn't want Crystal to see her using the library — "dealing with the enemy."

Finally at three o'clock, she saw them leave.

But now she had to face the new librarian. For some reason Bob terrified her.

The children's room was crowded. To Veronica's surprise, Bob jumped to his feet and ran out from behind his desk. He held the bar on the turnstile open for her.

He seemed pleased to see her.

"I'm glad you're back," he said. "I was afraid I had frightened you away. I promise I won't help you with any more problems."

Veronica suddenly felt at ease. "But I need problems," she said.

"You need problems?" Bob asked.

"Yes," Veronica said, "CHESS PROBLEMS."

"Did you say 'chess'?" Bob asked. "Do you play chess?"

"I'm just learning," Veronica said.

Bob was delighted. "I play chess myself."

Veronica suddenly realized she had entered a very special world.

"What books are you looking for?" Bob asked.

Veronica showed him the list of titles that Danny had suggested.

"Stay right here," Bob said. "I'll get them for you."

Veronica was not used to being waited on by the librarian. Bob set the two books on the table. "Do you mind if I point out a few others?"

"Not at all," Veronica said. "I need all the help I can get."

Bob brought over books and pointed out the sections of each book she might find helpful. Then he brought over books on the history of chess. It was clear that Bob loved everything about the game. Veronica began to get nervous.

"I have to learn in a hurry," she told Bob. "You see, my intended stepfather is coming to town this week for a tournament, and . . ."

"He's playing in the tournament this week?" Bob asked. "What's his name?"

"Count Carleton," Veronica said.

"If you'll excuse me a second," Bob said, "I'd like to look him up. Let me see. Count, Carleton."

Veronica sat at a table and waited. She suddenly realized she had not told Bob the Count's last name. She didn't even know it. But then she remembered that Bob was a librarian. He knew how to look things up. She just hoped he wouldn't make a big fuss about Carleton having a title.

She found herself wondering if Bob had any nice problem books that dealt with Child Phobia when Danny walked in.

He saw Veronica and came right over to the table.

"I was going to take those chess books out for you, but I see you got them." Danny reached into his bookbag. "Look, I brought you this." He put a folding chess set on the table. "You can borrow it."

Veronica didn't tell Danny about the expensive new chess set she was getting. She just said, "Thank you," and opened the board. She took out the chessmen and went over the names of the pieces. "Rook, bishop, knight, pawn . . ."

Danny looked surprised. "You have a good memory, Veronica," he said. "It helps in chess."

Veronica was pleased. "Danny, look," she whispered. "For various reasons I have to learn to play chess by tomorrow night and develop a profound knowledge of the game by Friday at seven o'clock. Do you think you could help me?"

Danny stared at Veronica.

Bob returned and pulled up a chair between Veronica and Danny. He had photocopies in his hand. He seemed very excited — so excited that his hands were shaking. Veronica felt a little embarrassed. She was sure it was because of Carleton being a Count.

Bob said, "Your stepfather . . ."

"Stepfather-to-be — " Veronica corrected him.

" — is listed in the World Chess Federation's directory as having a rating of 2500!"

"A rating of 2500?" Danny asked. "Are you serious? He's an international grand master! Wait until Chris hears about this."

"Not only that," Bob went on. "He seems to be the world expert on the Lowenthal Sicilian Defense."

Veronica was beginning to understand why, by accident, she had impressed the Count so much.

"He's coming for dinner on Friday," Veronica said, "and he wants to play chess with me."

"He wants to play chess with you?" Bob asked.

"Well, you see, he's never met me and he . . . um . . . has difficulty with children and I thought if I said I was interested in chess . . ."

"I see," Bob said, "you want to make him feel at ease — to break the ice . . . to show an interest in his hobby?"

Veronica nodded. "I don't have to win," she said.

"No danger of that," Bob said with a laugh.

Veronica was a little insulted. Deep down she hoped that, if she did win, the Count would be a good sport about it.

"You won't win," Danny whispered. "You can't possibly win. He's a grand master."

"What if I'm lucky?" Veronica asked.

"There is no such thing as luck in chess," Danny said. "It's all skill and experience. A beginner cannot defeat a grand master."

"I won't be a beginner by Friday," Veronica protested. "I'll know how to play chess by then."

"You will still be a beginner," Danny said. "You will be a beginner for months, probably years . . ."

Veronica suddenly felt very discouraged. She did not like being a beginner at anything. She was no longer so sure she wanted Danny's help. If he thought she had no chance of winning . . . if he didn't even have faith in her, he wouldn't make a good teacher. But Veronica was desperate.

"I'm a very fast learner," she said. It was true. Veronica was considered very bright at school.

Danny sighed and looked at the clock. "I have to be home exactly at six," he told Veronica. "We're going to my cousin's graduation party. I won't be back until tomorrow afternoon. But if it's all right with Bob, I could teach you some of the basics now. Would you like that?"

"Teach me," Veronica said. "Quick!"

Chapter 9

Mastering the Game

Bob told Danny it was fine with him if he taught Veronica chess in the library. In fact, he said he was delighted with the idea.

For the next two hours he quieted other children so that Danny and Veronica could concentrate. He tiptoed over with books and photocopies of some of the games the Count had played.

"You might study these sometime," Bob whispered, "but you'll have to learn to read the shorthand for recording chess moves. Actually there are two systems for recording chess moves — the old notation and the new."

"I'll learn both," Veronica promised.

Right from the start Danny was impressed with how quickly Veronica picked things up. The first time she set up the chessboard, she set it up perfectly without any help from him.

Danny was startled. "That's amazing, Veronica. You even have the queens on color."

"Huh?" Veronica asked.

"Well, you have all the pieces lined up right, the rooks, the knights, the bishops . . . the pawns in front, but the trick is making sure the white queen is on a white square and the black queen on black. How did you know to do that?"

Veronica had an eerie feeling. "I don't know," she said. "It just felt right."

"Maybe someone showed you when you were little," Danny suggested. "Do it again."

Veronica did it again. Perfectly.

"Capablanca did that," Danny said. "When he was only five years old. He set up the chessboard perfectly right away. Then he beat his father the first time he played. He was a child prodigy."

"Who is Capablanca?" Veronica asked,

wondering if she were already too old to be considered a child prodigy.

"One of the most famous chess players who ever lived," Danny said.

Danny showed Veronica how each piece moved. In no time at all she had it.

"Bishops move on the diagonal, rooks on the straight, the queen can move on the straight and the diagonal as many squares as she likes. . . ."

"Right," Danny said, "so the queen is your most powerful piece — most valuable, too."

Veronica even learned the knight's move, which was the hardest — two squares in one direction, and one to the side. "Like the letter L," Danny told her.

Veronica had never concentrated so hard in her life. When she had learned the moves, she looked down at the board of sixty-four checkered squares, with the chessmen lined up like two opposing armies ready for battle, and said, "Can we play now?"

"Not yet," Danny said. "Now you have to learn how each chessman captures an enemy chessman. It is not always the same way they move. As you know, a pawn moves straight ahead, but only one square at a time. . . ."

"It can move two squares on its first move of the game," Veronica added quickly, "and it is not allowed to move backwards."

"Right," Danny said. "But a pawn can capture only on the diagonal."

"Like this?"

"Yes," Danny said.

"Now we play!" Veronica said happily.

Danny smiled at Veronica. "Well, maybe I should show you the object of the game."

"Oh, I already know that." Veronica was a little impatient. "Whoever captures the most enemy pieces wins."

"No," Danny said. "The object of the game is to 'checkmate' the enemy king . . . to trap the king so there is no place that he can move without being captured."

"That's nice," Veronica said, tapping her fingers on the table. "Let's play."

"Well, maybe that would be a good idea," Danny said. "Then you'll see what I'm talking about."

Veronica set up the board.

"You take white and I'll take black," Danny said. "White always goes first, so white has the advantage."

"I would rather have black," Veronica said. She wanted to see what Danny would do first. "Good strategy in war," she told herself.

Danny moved the white pawn in front of his king ahead two squares.

Veronica, using her Fast Attack Theory, copied his move. With lightning speed, she pushed the pawn in front of the black king ahead two squares. The two pawns were facing each other.

"Excellent, Veronica," Danny said. "That's a good opening move. You want to control the center of the board. This is called the king's pawn opening."

Veronica didn't see what difference it made what it was called. She watched as Danny moved the pawn in front of his king's bishop ahead two squares and set it down right next to his other pawn.

Veronica was about to do the same thing when she suddenly stopped and stared at the board. She couldn't believe Danny was making a mistake like this. Was it fair to just take his pawn without warning him first?

"Danny," Veronica said slowly, "I know you're never allowed to take back a move in chess once you've touched a piece, but . . ."

"But what?" Danny asked. "What's the matter?"

"Well, it's okay with me if you take back your move."

"Why would I want to do that?" Danny was surprised.

"Danny," Veronica whispered. "Your pawn is in checkmate."

"Only a king can be in checkmate," Danny said. He seemed puzzled.

"Well, if you leave the pawn where it is, I will take it with my pawn . . . right there on the diagonal." Veronica couldn't believe Danny hadn't noticed that. Danny had played chess since he was seven years old.

"I know you'll probably take it," Danny explained. "It's called a gambit. A gambit means a sacrifice. I'm going to let you take that pawn."

Veronica was suspicious. "Are you going to take my pawn?" she asked. But she didn't see how he could.

"Sometimes you sacrifice a piece to strengthen your position," Danny said.

Veronica stared in horror at Danny.

"I can't take a helpless pawn," she said.

"Well, you don't have to if you don't want to," Danny said slowly. "It would then be called the king's gambit declined."

Veronica had a feeling that chess was a much simpler game than people thought. It was just that there were so many fancy names for things. . . .

But something else was bothering her.

"*I* would never sacrifice a pawn," Veronica said. "It simply isn't right."

"Huh?" Danny said.

Veronica was beginning to feel quite emotional about it. "A pawn is a poor foot soldier, right? Never had a chance in his life. Meanwhile, you have this rich queen running around the board wherever she likes and does she care one little bit about the pawn?" Veronica's voice had risen. "Or about the pawn's family?"

"Um . . . Veronica . . ."

"I would rather sacrifice a queen any day," Veronica announced. "In fact, she deserves it."

"But . . ." Danny turned and looked out the window. He seemed deep in thought. Veronica hoped he was changing his mind about the way he had been treating pawns all these years.

"I'm calling Chris," Danny suddenly said. "Do you mind if I tell him about the Count being a grand master?"

"Oh, please tell him," Veronica said.

Veronica waited for Danny and thought with pleasure about the speed with which she was learning chess. "I'm way ahead of schedule," she told herself. "I can start working on my profound knowledge tonight."

Veronica had always suspected that she might be a genius. Maybe that's what Danny was telling Chris right this minute.

She wandered over to the shelves to see if there were any chess books about Equal Rights for Pawns. She noticed a book called *Chess Psychology*, which sounded interesting for an advanced player, so she added that to her pile of chess books.

Danny returned looking confused.

"Did you tell Chris about the Count?" Veronica asked. "Did you tell him how I was doing?"

Danny nodded. "Chris said I wasn't allowed to show you anything more about chess."

"Why not?" Veronica asked.

"He said it would interfere with your training. He said he was taking over as your chess coach."

"My coach?" Veronica thought that sounded very impressive. But Danny looked so unhappy, she said, "Can't you both teach me?"

Danny shrugged. "That's what I said, but Chris said he's been your friend longer than I have."

"My friend?" Veronica asked. "Are you sure that's what he said?"

Chris always treated her like a pest who just happened to live across the hall. "Are you sure he said 'friend'?"

"Well, maybe he said he has known you much longer. He said he knows how your mind works and he doesn't want you looking at any chess books until he approves them."

"How silly," Veronica said, but she felt secretly pleased to think Danny and Chris were fighting over who was going to teach her.

Danny sat down and stared miserably at the chessboard. "Chris wants to start coaching you right away."

Veronica felt sorry for Danny. She knew how it felt to be jealous. "You don't mind if he teaches me a few little details, do you?"

"He doesn't want to teach you," Danny said nervously. "He wants to be your coach."

Veronica thought about that. A coach was someone who worked with a player who already knew a game . . . someone who already had talent.

Bob tiptoed over with another chess book.

"I hate to interrupt," he said, "but you two might be interested in learning about an old French poem called 'Les Echecs Amoureux.'"

"What does that mean?" Danny asked.

"It means 'Loving Chess.' It was written in the fourteenth century during the Age of Chivalry. In this poem a knight crusader addresses his lady love and teaches her to play chess to distract her from the attentions of his rivals. . . ."

Danny glanced at Veronica and looked away quickly. His face was bright red. Veronica pretended not to have heard. She didn't want to embarrass Danny.

Danny mumbled, "I wish I wasn't going away. . . ."

"That's all right," Veronica said. "I promise I won't let Chris show me anything until you get back."

Veronica was beginning to wonder if there was all that much more for her to learn. She decided she would spend tonight reading *Chess Psychology* . . . maybe work on a few theories that might interest the Count. . . .

"I'm sorry I can't help you get these books home," Danny said, "but I'll be late."

"I'll help her carry them," said a cheerful voice.

Veronica turned around.

"Crystal!" she said.

Chapter 10

The Right Atmosphere

"I guess Bob just wants to help people," Veronica said to Crystal on the way home.

"He asked us if we knew you," Crystal said. "He was afraid he had scared you away."

"How did you know I went to the library?" Veronica asked.

"I called and your mother told me."

They walked for a few blocks in silence.

"I'm sorry I called you a traitor," Veronica said.

Crystal nodded, but she didn't say anything. Veronica felt uncomfortable.

"Did you get the book about Baby Ruth?" Veronica asked politely.

"Babe Ruth," Crystal murmured. "He was a baseball player. Yes, I got it."

"You see, I had to go to the library," Veronica explained. "It was an emergency. I had to research chess."

"Why are you suddenly so interested in chess?" Crystal asked. "I thought chess was boring."

"Oh, no!" Veronica said. "It's the most exciting game in the world. Romantic, too."

Veronica told Crystal about the Count coming for dinner, and how she had to help her mother get her marriage proposal back. . . .

Crystal sighed. "Veronica, are you still trying to be a matchmaker?"

Veronica was quiet. If Crystal didn't believe in anything she said, she wasn't going to talk about her private life anymore. Besides, she was ashamed to admit her father had gotten married behind her back.

Chris was waiting at the corner of the block. "Veronica," he said. "What took you so long? I was getting worried."

"You were worried about me?" Veronica stared down at Chris. Chris was shorter than both

Veronica and Crystal. He was wearing a red-and-white-striped shirt and white pants. His hair was combed. Veronica found herself thinking that Chris and Danny were both very handsome in their different ways.

"You were worried about Veronica?" Crystal asked.

"Oh, hi, Crystal," Chris said. "I can't watch the baseball game with you tonight. Something important came up." He gave Veronica a meaningful look.

Chris took Veronica's elbow and pulled her aside. "I'm bringing in an expert," he whispered.

"An expert?" Veronica asked.

"To advise me as your chess coach," Chris explained. "I'm on my way to see him right now." He noticed the stack of library books.

Chris groaned. "Oh, no, Veronica. Promise me you won't even look at those books until I see them. Where did you get that folding chess set?"

"Danny lent it to me," Veronica said.

Chris was annoyed. "Oh, he did, did he? Well, don't touch it!" Veronica was surprised that Chris would be so jealous.

"What's going on?" Crystal asked when Chris had gone. "Chris is acting strange."

Veronica didn't say anything.

Crystal was curious. "What made you say chess was romantic?"

Veronica had no intention of discussing the difficulty of *almost* being in the middle of a love triangle. She didn't trust Crystal anymore. She was afraid their friendship would never be the same.

Crystal helped Veronica carry the books into her apartment. There was a telegram for her on the front hall table. Veronica rested the books on the table and stared at the telegram.

"Aren't you going to open it?" Crystal asked.

Veronia opened it. Right away she was sorry she had. It was from her father.

DEAR VERONICA: WE HOPE YOU ARE ALL RIGHT. WE THOUGHT YOU WOULD BE PLEASED WITH THE NEWS. . . .

"We?" Veronica was outraged. The father that had been hers alone was now calling himself "we."

Crystal was watching her. "It's nothing

important," Veronica said and she put the telegram back in the envelope.

Crystal said, "Look, Veronica, I wish I could help you more. I just don't know anything about chess. But, if you ever need anything else — a bridesmaid, for instance — remember I'm right next door."

Veronica thought that was a very nice thing to say. She just stood there for a moment, wishing that Crystal would stay. Then she said, "Crystal, I don't have an immediate need for a bridesmaid anymore, well, at least I don't need one for my father. . . ."

Veronica told Crystal how her father and Chloe got married in city hall yesterday — "At least, I think he married Chloe. . . ."

"What?" Crystal was shocked. "He got married without telling you?"

Veronica was embarrassed. "Oh, you know, my father doesn't like to make a big fuss about things. It doesn't really bother me."

Crystal didn't seem to know what to say. "I'll help you put these books in your room," she murmured.

When Veronica went to pile the books on her desk, she ran into a problem. Her desk wasn't there. She looked around. Her bed was missing. The curtains were gone, and so was the rug. In fact, her room was bare, except for cardboard boxes that had her toys and books in them.

Crystal was standing behind her. She gasped. "Veronica, are you moving?"

"I don't think so," Veronica said.

"Oh, Veronica, I hope you're not upset, but I got the most wonderful idea. . . ."

Veronica turned and saw her mother standing in the doorway. She looked extremely youthful in a light blue denim jumpsuit.

"Well, I finally get to meet Crystal Webb," Elaine Schmidt said with a smile. "Excuse the mess. I got that nice young man on the second floor to help me move things around. He and his friend are coming back to bring in the bookshelves from the living room. The Oriental rug should arrive in a little while. I thought we'd see how it looked in here."

"The Oriental rug is going in here?" Veronica asked.

"The chess table, too, but it won't be delivered until Monday. The pieces have to be very carefully packed. I also got this wonderful standing lamp with a map of the ancient world on the shade. I thought we'd move the leather armchair in here and my antique desk, too. The living room will be less cluttered. And, you know, Veronica, that leather armchair turns into the most comfortable little bed."

"Is it still my room?"

"Of course it is, darling, and we can move everything back if you don't like it. We put all your furniture in the storage room in the basement. But I figured since you will be leaving for Santa Barbara in three weeks, you wouldn't mind. . . ."

"Oh, Veronica!" Crystal burst out. "Don't you get it? Your room will have so much atmosphere . . . books lining the wall, the armchair and the chess table . . . I can just see the fog rolling in and the old grandfather clock in the corner ticking away the hours until the stroke of midnight. . . ."

Elaine Schmidt looked at Crystal with delight. "That's just what I had in mind," she said. "I was thinking it would be like the drawing room of an old English manor in a murder mystery story."

"Bloodstains on the rug," Crystal agreed.

Elaine Schmidt laughed. "I don't know about that, but I like the idea of the grandfather clock ticking away in the corner."

Veronica was thrilled. The plans for redecorating her room appealed to her. She could picture herself seated in the leather armchair concentrating on a complicated chess problem with Gulliver on her lap. The maid would serve her tea. . . .

"I don't mind at all," Veronica said. "We can keep it that way." She had decided to wait and surprise her mother with the news that she was not going to Santa Barbara this summer. She thought for a moment. "So, after we have dinner on Friday, we retire to the drawing room to play chess, right?"

"It sounds so *elegant*!" Crystal said. "Can I help? I could move the books in here."

"As a matter of fact, I was just about to ask your mother if you could stay for dinner," Veronica's mother said. "Have you ever had fondue?"

Crystal shook her head. "But I'd love to try it."

Veronica did not have time to study chess that evening. The Oriental rug arrived. It was a magnificent deep blue with a white-and-gold pattern. The three of them arranged the books in the dark wooden bookshelves and brought in the leather chair and the antique desk. It looked wonderful.

Scene I: (Veronica told herself) Veronica's Drawing Room. Enter the Count . . .

Then they had dinner.

Veronica had never had fondue, either. They each got to cook their own pieces of beef with a long fork in a pot full of boiling broth. The pot sat on the dining room table with a candle under it. Then they had a choice of different sauces to dip the beef in. Veronica loved it.

For dessert they had cherries jubilee.

Veronica had never been so proud of her mother in her whole life.

Crystal asked her mother all sorts of questions about Europe. After dinner her mother showed them slides of Italy and Greece.

"Your mother is so adventurous!" Crystal

whispered to Veronica. "I want to be like her when I grow up."

Chris came to the door three times. Veronica was surprised. Chris never knocked on her door except on Halloween when he was trick-or-treating.

The first time, he just wanted to tell Veronica that he had had a successful meeting with the expert. "Don't worry about a thing," he said.

The second time, he said that he would be her half-brother's god-brother, until he found out that Veronica had been talking about her father's child, not the Count's.

The third time he did not ask to see Veronica.

"He wanted to let me know that he had no plans for Friday evening," Elaine Schmidt said. "I wonder what he meant by that."

Chapter 11

No, Gulliver!

The leather chair turned into a very comfortable bed, but Veronica did not sleep well. The shadows in her room were different. Gulliver did not sleep curled up on her feet as he usually did. He seemed disturbed by the changes in the room.

Veronica had a strange dream. She was on a giant chessboard and only allowed to move along the diagonal on the black squares — just like a bishop. But every time she tried to step on a black square, it turned white.

The next morning she woke up late and looked around for Gulliver. Gulliver was in a corner, pawing the new rug. Veronica tumbled out of bed and swooped up Gulliver in her arms. "No, Gulliver!" she whispered. "Don't do that!"

Gulliver had never scratched the furniture. He was not able to scratch furniture. Her mother had had his claws removed. He had always been a very well-behaved cat. To Veronica's surprise, Gulliver was shaking. She let him go and he ran wildly around the room as if something was after him.

Then she noticed the dark stain in the corner of the rug. She sniffed the air. It was a warm humid day outside, and there was a faint smell of cat urine in the air. Veronica didn't know what to do. Gulliver had always used the kitty litter box in the bathroom off Veronica's room.

She caught Gulliver and put him in the bathroom and closed the door behind him. She studied the wet spot on the rug. She was about to get some soap and water and a scrub brush when she remembered that her mother had said that an Oriental rug had to be cleaned. "It will go away," she told herself, "as soon as it dries."

"Veronica!" her mother called. "Are you awake? Crystal is here, and we want to ask you something."

Veronica put on her bathrobe and opened all the windows so the smell would go away. She closed the door to her room so the smell wouldn't be noticed in the rest of the apartment.

Veronica was a bit surprised to find Crystal and her mother having breakfast together in the dining room. "We were just talking about Gulliver," her mother said. Veronica could hear Gulliver mewing and pounding at her bathroom door.

"Crystal was telling me that a person who is allergic to cats can have an allergic reaction even if the cat isn't there," her mother said. "We will need a few days at least to clean up the hairs and get rid of the cat presence in the apartment before Carleton comes."

Veronica glanced at Crystal. She did not like the idea of Crystal and her mother discussing *her* cat.

"I spoke to your grandfather a little while ago, and he said it would be all right with him if

Gulliver spent a week with him in Vermont. We could send him up there this afternoon."

"No!" Veronica said. "I'd rather he stay at Chris's." At least she would be able to see him every day. Her poodle, Lady Jane Grey, always spent the summers in Vermont, but Veronica could not live without Gulliver.

"I'll have to speak to Chris's mother. Five days is a long time," her mother said. "I have a feeling Gulliver and Tiger fought the last time."

Crystal said, "I wish we could take him, but my mother won't let a cat in the house. Gabriella is afraid of cats." Gabriella was her mother's dog — a spoiled little Pomeranian.

Veronica ate her breakfast. Her mother had made Belgian waffles. Gulliver had quieted down, but when Veronica went to check on him, she found he had escaped from the bathroom and was once again pawing the rug.

"No, Gulliver!" Veronica picked up Gulliver and carried him with her to the kitchen.

Her mother and Crystal were putting the dishes in the dishwasher together.

"I asked Crystal if she'd help you sort through

some of your old toys and clothes today, so we could get rid of those boxes," her mother said. "I'm sure there are plenty of things you could throw out."

Crystal was looking at Veronica. Veronica had not been planning to throw anything out, but she shrugged. "I guess so."

"And Chris came by and asked if you could go over there this evening. He said something about wanting you to meet an expert. What kind of expert?"

"A chess expert," Veronica said.

"Well, it's funny, but I told your grandfather how impressed Carleton had been with your knowledge of chess, and he said he remembers teaching you chess when you were only three years old."

"Really?" Veronica asked. "Was I good?"

"You'll have to ask him," her mother said with a smile. "It's quite a startling story."

Veronica was sure she must have beaten her grandfather.

* * *

"Veronica, do you really need this old polar bear with no eyes?" Crystal asked. She was giggling.

Veronica nodded stiffly. She had refused to throw out anything except a Little Golden Book that had no cover and big orange crayon marks on each page that went back to a period before Veronica learned to "respect books."

Veronica sat in the leather chair holding on tightly to Gulliver.

Crystal picked up a ragged stuffed monkey and held it up. Then she stopped and looked at Veronica.

"I like the chair better where it was," Crystal said. "I don't understand why you moved it."

"I like it here and it's my room," Veronica said crossly.

Veronica was trapped. The chair had to stay where it was. She had moved it to cover the stain that now had turned into a yellowing patch on the blue Oriental rug. Spraying her mother's best toilet water on the spot had not disguised the odor. Veronica knew it was just a matter of time. Gulliver was a doomed cat.

At two o'clock her mother came in to see how they were doing, and Veronica could see her delicate nose crinkle up. "What's that smell?" she asked. "Why did you move the chair?"

Elaine Schmidt never lost her temper. She just made a few telephone calls.

At four o'clock Gulliver was picked up by Animal Transport Carriers and taken to the airport.

"But Gulliver's not a country cat," Veronica said to her mother. "He doesn't even have claws to defend himself in Vermont."

"Gulliver's not going to Vermont," her mother said. "I had a much better idea. It will work out beautifully, and your father said it would be fine with them. He'll pick Gulliver up at the airport, and Gulliver will be comfortably settled by the time you get out to Santa Barbara."

"What if I don't want to go to Santa Barbara?" Veronica asked her mother. "What if I want to spend the summer with you?"

"But, darling, I won't be here. I'll be in the Greek islands."

Chapter 12

A Natural Talent

Veronica wrote another letter:

Dear Lorenzo:
    You will soon get my letter about not coming to Santa Barbara. Please have the courtesy to return my cat this Saturday without fail.
                    Sincerdy,
                    Veronica

She had it all figured out. She and Gulliver would spend a nice quiet summer alone in the apartment. She had done it many times before. In fact, this was the first time she had been invited to spend the summer with her father. Barbara would be there, so her mother wouldn't worry. She would devote herself to chess. . . .

But when Barbara returned from her weekend, Veronica learned that her mother had given her notice.

"She fired me," Barbara said cheerfully as Veronica watched her pack. "I was going to quit anyway. Your mother tells me she is planning to get a maid."

"Are we really getting a maid?" Veronica asked her mother.

"The agency is sending some people over tomorrow for me to interview," her mother told her. "We certainly will need a maid to serve Friday evening."

Veronica didn't mind the idea of spending the summer with Gulliver and a maid.

Veronica shut herself into her room with her chess books. She was sure that in a very short time, her memory of being a child prodigy would come back to her. She could just picture the expression on her grandfather's face when he was beaten by a three-year-old!

She was delighted to find that the autobiography of José Raúl Capablanca was among the books Bob had selected for her. She decided to do her book report on the famous chess player. She already knew how she would start. "It is not easy to be a genius . . ." she would write.

Veronica took her poodle out for a walk. When she got back, she retrieved her Little Golden Book from the garbage in the hallway. It occurred to her that someone someday might be interested in the early scribblings of a world-famous chess player. . . . When she passed the kitchen door to Chris's apartment, she saw it was open. She could hear Chris talking. "What's the matter, Tiger?"

He was talking to his cat. Veronica suddenly missed Gulliver very much.

To her surprise, she heard a strange crackly voice answer, "Oh, I'm all right. Just a little tired, I guess."

Veronica gasped. Then she realized that Chris was not only talking to his cat, he was answering for his cat. Veronica tiptoed away. She was sure it was not a conversation Chris would like anyone to overhear. But just at that moment, Chris came out. "Veronica!" he said.

"I just got here," Veronica said quickly.

"Come over as soon as you finish dinner. The expert says it would be helpful if you learned the new notation system — the algebraic."

Veronica was curious to meet the expert. "I'll try," she said. "Will Danny be there?"

"We don't need Danny," Chris said crossly. "Besides, he's against our plan."

"What plan?" Veronica asked.

"Veronica," Chris said, "the expert has a chess computer. It plays on a very high level."

Playing against a computer might be fun, Veronica thought, but . . .

"I won't come unless Danny is there," Veronica said. After all, she had promised Danny.

Chris sighed. "I'll call him."

Veronica told her mother she wasn't hungry and spent the time learning the shorthand for recording chess moves. She opened Danny's chessboard and taught herself both systems — the old and the new.

The new system looked difficult at first, but then she realized that each square on the board had been assigned a letter of the alphabet and a number. In two hours she had broken the code. She wasn't the least bit surprised.

"Danny will be a little late," Chris said.

Veronica was disappointed to find out the expert was only Peter, a friend of Chris's. Peter had never been very fond of Veronica.

To her surprise, the first thing Peter said was, "I like the way you are wearing your hair. It looks nice tucked back on one side like that and covering the other ear."

"Keep it that way," Chris said.

Veronica blushed and wondered why she was suddenly getting so much attention from boys.

Chris and Peter played a game of chess. Veronica called out the moves and wrote them down. Chris and Peter were impressed with how quickly and accurately Veronica had learned the notation system. Veronica felt good.

"Excellent, Veronica," Chris said. "You can just relax until Friday." He stood up and walked her to the door.

"But I thought you wanted to see how I played against a computer," Veronica said.

"That won't be necessary," Chris said. "We're not going to use the computer until Friday night."

Veronica felt nervous. She wished Danny would arrive.

"I don't get it," Veronica said.

"It's simple," Peter said. "We're going to wire you."

"Wire me?" Veronica stared at Chris.

Chris was excited. "We'll use Peter's walkie-talkies and we'll hide this tiny earphone under your hair. . . ."

"Keep your hair exactly the way it is," Peter said.

"Peter will be in the hallway with the chess computer and a walkie-talkie," Chris went on. "I will be sitting with you and the Count. I will also have a walkie-talkie hidden in my pocket. I will call off the Count's moves — out loud, of course

— and Peter will be able to hear each move over his walkie-talkie."

"I'll punch them into the computer," Peter continued, "and read off what the computer tells you to do next. You'll hear it over the tiny earphone and do exactly what the computer tells you to do."

"Like a robot?" Veronica asked.

"Not *exactly* a robot," Chris said.

Veronica looked from Chris to Peter. She felt like crying. "But that's cheating!"

Chris groaned. "You can't win anyway. I'm sure he can beat the computer, even though it plays on a very high level. But at least you won't look like a fool."

Veronica was shocked. "What makes you think I'll look like a fool? Didn't Danny tell you how quickly I learned to play? Didn't he tell you about my *natural talent*?"

Chris didn't say anything. He just looked down at the floor. "Well, didn't he tell you?" Veronica demanded.

"He told me you were having trouble understanding the game," Chris mumbled.

"How ridiculous!" Veronica was furious. "I didn't have any trouble at all. I understand chess perfectly. He probably just didn't agree with my theories."

"Theories?" Peter asked.

The doorbell rang. "That's Danny," Chris said.

"Good," Veronica said. "I have something to give him."

Veronica wouldn't even look at Danny. "Wait here," she said. She marched past him, went to her apartment, and got the folding chess set he had lent her.

When she got back, Danny said, "Veronica, I'm so glad you said no. I was against wiring you. I promise I'll help you every afternoon this week."

"No, thank you," Veronica said coldly. "I won't be needing your help." She handed him his folding chess set. "I won't be needing this. I will be getting a professional chess set."

Danny seemed very surprised.

"I wasn't fooled," Veronica went on. "I am well aware that the only reason Chris was being nice to me was so he could meet the Count, and Peter just wanted to try out his walkie-talkies on me, but you're the worst. . . ."

"I am?" Danny asked.

"Yes. You were being nice to me *for no reason*." Veronica paused so that Danny would feel the full force of that accusation. Then she said as calmly as she could, "Someday you will be very sorry you told Chris I didn't understand the game."

"But you will understand the game," Danny said. "You just have to be a little patient."

"I already understand it," Veronica said. "All I have to do is refresh my memory. It so happens my grandfather taught me chess when I was three years old. It is a startling story."

And with that, Veronica returned to her drawing room to bury herself in her books.

She opened *Chess Psychology* and closed out everything else. "Know your opponent," it began.

Chapter 13

Proof

On Monday Kimberly turned to Veronica during study hall. "Veronica," she whispered, "I looked up how to address a count in my mother's etiquette book and there's something wrong."

Veronica was trying to read a book about chess. "What's wrong?" Veronica asked.

"Is the Count from England?" Kimberly asked.

"I guess so," Veronica said. Carleton sounded like an English name.

"Well, he can't be," Kimberly snapped. "There is no such thing as an English count. There are countesses, but they are the wives of earls."

"Well, then he's from someplace else," Veronica mumbled.

"Veronica," Kimberly said in a warning voice, "it's not for me. It's Amy who needs proof."

Veronica was too busy trying to understand the difference between opening games, middle games, and end games.

The new chess set did not arrive that afternoon.

"One of the pieces was defective," her mother told her. "They've ordered another set and they promise me it will arrive by Thursday at the latest."

This did not worry Veronica. She had read that a great chess player could picture a whole chessboard in his mind. He could see all the moves and the combinations of moves. He didn't need to have a real chessboard in front of him.

"It will be good practice," she told herself.

Veronica spent a few minutes memorizing the first two moves of a chess game. She closed her eyes. To her amazement, she could indeed visualize the entire chessboard after each move.

Not only that! She could see the white wicker table the chessboard was standing on . . . a vase of cornflowers sitting on the table, and two glasses of pink lemonade. It was a lazy summer day, and she could hear the porch swing creaking. . . .

Veronica opened her eyes at once. She felt a terrible shudder come over her. What was happening? She closed her eyes again. Now she could see the pattern of dots on the milky-white vase that held the cornflowers. She could smell strawberries. Every detail on the porch was sharp and clear. . . .

There was only one problem. She had never seen that porch in her entire life!

Veronica couldn't figure out what was happening, but it frightened her. She was in no hurry to call up any more visions of chessboards.

She spent the rest of Monday evening with her mother in the living room. Her mother showed her a present Carleton had given her.

It was an old book called *Flora's Dictionary*, published in 1855. "The language of flowers?" Veronica asked.

Her mother nodded. She was blushing. "Are you going to laugh?" she asked.

Veronica promised not to laugh.

"The day after we met, Carleton sent me a bunch of purple lilacs."

Veronica looked up purple lilacs. " 'The first emotions of love,' " she whispered. "Oh, Mama!"

"And when he proposed, he brought a dozen of the most beautiful red roses I've ever seen. . . ."

Red roses were a declaration of love — a clear and simple message.

"May I show this to Crystal?" Veronica begged her mother.

"I don't see why not." Her mother smiled.

Crystal was fascinated by the little book. "I can't believe it," she said. "Yellow roses are my favorite, but guess what they mean."

"What?" Veronica asked.

" 'A decrease in love'!"

Veronica was enjoying the week alone with her mother. Her mother looked radiant and happy. "It will be nice to see Carleton again," she said. She asked Veronica's advice on everything: the menu, what she should wear. . . . They read *Amy Vanderbilt's Etiquette Book* together, and Veronica brushed up on her manners.

"Will there be bones in the fish?" Veronica asked.

"I hope not," her mother said.

Veronica skipped the chapter on how to choke politely on fish bones.

On Tuesday Veronica was introduced to Marion, the maid who would be coming on Friday. She seemed like a pleasant, comfortable woman, but "Marion doesn't allow children in the kitchen," her mother told her.

"Just on Friday, right?" Veronica could not imagine spending the whole summer not being allowed in the kitchen. "It's just for the dinner party, right?"

"Well, of course," her mother said.

Every day that week a letter arrived from her father. Veronica glanced at one and saw the word "we" all over the page. She folded it up again in a hurry. She did not have the time for people who were living happily ever after without her.

She hoped he would be a little disappointed to

hear she was not coming to Santa Barbara.

On Wednesday there were telephone messages from her father. "He said he got two letters from you. He wants you to call him right away," her mother said.

"Did he tell you what was in the letters?" Veronica asked.

"Of course not," her mother said. "That's between you and Lorenzo. But please call him. He sounded worried."

Veronica did not call her father. Instead, she practiced moving quietly and smoothly around the apartment so that she wouldn't scare the Count by sudden childish movements.

When her father called late that night, Veronica pretended to be asleep.

During study hall on Thursday, she wrote down the most grown-up conversations she could think up so that the Count would not have an attack of Child Phobia.

"How does this sound?" she asked Crystal and she read off a list of intelligent questions on investment banking and a few thoughtful remarks on the state of world affairs.

"I don't know," Crystal said. "It sounds a little dull."

"Well, mostly we'll be talking about chess theories," Veronica said.

Kimberly was watching them. Veronica was beginning to wish that she did have some proof about the Count. Amy had been talking behind her back all week.

Veronica's book report on the life of Capablanca was hanging on the bulletin board. Veronica was now very sorry she had begun it with the words "It is not easy to be a genius."

Amy had really enjoyed that. She told everyone in the school that Veronica thought *she* was a genius.

The chessboard still hadn't arrived. "They promised it by tomorrow morning," her mother said.

Veronica stayed up late Thursday night reading about chess, but every time she saw a chessboard appear before her eyes, she stopped and tried to think about something else. She could not call up a chessboard without also calling up the strange vision of the wicker table and the cornflowers.

She found an article Bob had copied from *Who's Who* about the Count and began to read.

Suddenly she realized she had proof. Veronica dialed Kimberly's number and told her. "He's in reference books because he's famous," Veronica told her. "He's in *Who's Who*."

"My mother has *Who's Who*." Kimberly sounded happy. "I'll show it to Amy tomorrow morning when she comes to pick me up."

Veronica put on her nightgown and got into bed. She began to read. The print was small. Veronica was tired.

Then she noticed the typo. It was right in the first line of the article in *Who's Who*. Veronica looked at another biography of the Count in *Who's Who in Chess*. She was surprised that they had made the same mistake. But her eyes kept closing. She was too tired to go on reading. She fell asleep with the articles next to her pillow.

Chapter 14

Count Comma

In the middle of the night Veronica woke up in a cold sweat. She had had a terrible dream.

Once again she was on a giant chessboard, but she wasn't able to move at all. She wasn't safe on any square.

Both armies — the white chessmen and the black — were attacking her. Even her friends the pawns were shooting at her, and their weapons were most unusual.

They were shooting punctuation.

Veronica was wounded in the leg with a semicolon and struck on the back of her neck with an exclamation point. But then she saw the most deadly weapon of all heading right for her. It was a comma!

Veronica turned on the lamp. She reached for the article from *Who's Who*.

There it was:

Count, Carleton. Born in Sweetwater, Oklahoma. Mother's name: Maida Dixon Count . . .

Count Comma Carleton. Count was his last name.

Carleton Count.

"But you didn't lie," Crystal said on the bus the next morning. "You didn't lie because you honestly believed he was a count."

"I wanted to believe that," Veronica said calmly. "I lied to myself — I didn't even know it. That's worse than lying on purpose."

Crystal said slowly, "No, I don't think it is."

"It's the worst kind of lie," Veronica went on. This morning Veronica was studying everything with a clear critical eye — including herself. "I fooled myself," she said.

Crystal was impressed. "I never heard you talk that way before."

"Chess sharpens the mind," Veronica said dryly. "It is very important to see your own position clearly when confronting the opponent."

Veronica had read those words the night before in *Chess Psychology*.

"Now I have every reason to believe," Veronica went on without emotion, "that Amy will attack me as soon as I arrive at school, call me a liar, which will be shortly followed by ridicule, whispering behind my back, and referring to me by such nicknames as Veronica the Show-off — the Countess, perhaps. . . ."

Veronica was almost beginning to enjoy this brilliant analysis of her own predicament when she looked out the window and saw Amy, Kimberly, and their friends standing on the steps of Maxton Academy.

Veronica said thoughtfully, "Maybe I'll just stay on the bus."

"Don't worry, Veronica," Crystal whispered. "I'll be right next to you all day."

But Crystal didn't have a chance. As soon as the bus came to a stop, the group of girls came tearing down the school steps. When Veronica stepped off the bus, she was surrounded. Amy got to her first.

"We're in love with him," Amy announced.

"In love with who?" Veronica asked.

"With your stepfather, of course," Amy said.

"The Count!" Kimberly said. "Who else? Oh, Veronica, he looks so cute when he's thinking!"

"He's not a count," Veronica said. "Count is his last name. His name is Carleton Count."

"I know that," Kimberly said. "He's just called 'the Count' by the newspapers. My father says an international grand master is a much higher title than a count anyway. My father says he is going to win the tournament."

Veronica felt confused. She looked at Ashley, a quiet girl she trusted more than the others.

Ashley was studying Veronica with cool gray eyes.

"Veronica," she said. "Didn't you see this morning's paper?"

Chapter 15

Enter the Count

Carleton Count (known as "the Count") has exquisite manners, a gentle appearance, and a taste for rare books on poetry, music, and flowers.

But, in the chess world, he is considered a brilliant and ruthless opponent.

Veronica looked at the photograph in the newspaper. Her future stepfather was studying a chessboard. The tips of his long graceful fingers were poised on his temples, and his dark eyes were half-closed, hidden by thick, dark lashes. He had fine features, long, wavy dark hair that fell over his forehead, a thin, sensitive mouth, and a strong chin.

"He looks so dashing," Crystal said. "He looks like someone from another century."

Veronica was happy that she had spent so much time brushing up on her manners.

On the way home from school, the sky turned dark and it began to rain. Crystal and Veronica began to run.

Chris and Danny were outside her building, setting up a lemonade stand on the sidewalk under the canopy. "In the rain?" Crystal asked.

Veronica tried to slip into the building, but Chris stopped her.

"Did you know that Carleton Count won the chess tournament?" Chris asked.

"He did?" Veronica asked. She was no longer angry at either Chris or Danny.

"We have to buy him tulips," Crystal said. "Flora says that tulips mean fame."

Veronica thought that was an excellent idea. She and Crystal went around the corner and bought a bunch of tulips. It was raining harder.

"By the way, what time is he coming to dinner?"

Chris asked when they passed the stand again.

"Seven o'clock." Veronica said. Suddenly she felt bad.

"I'm sorry I can't invite you and Danny to meet the Count, but, you see, it's supposed to be a romantic dinner, and he gets a little nervous around children."

"That's okay," Chris said.

"How are you doing at chess?" Danny asked.

"Well, I've been doing a lot of reading," Veronica said.

"Do you have any questions?" Danny asked.

Veronica thought about that. "No," she said, "but I do have some new opinions."

Danny looked worried. "How do you like your new chess set?" he asked.

"I haven't actually seen it yet," Veronica told him, "but it should be upstairs right now."

"Do you mean you were without a chess set all week?" Danny asked.

"I didn't really need it," Veronica said. "I can see the moves in my head."

"Really?" Danny asked. "Can you see part of the board or the entire board?"

Veronica knew that some of the greatest chess players could only envision part of the board.

"The entire board," Veronica said. "It's scary."

"Scary?" Danny asked. "Wait a minute. How many moves can you see ahead?"

Veronica was puzzled. "Ahead? Oh, I see what you mean. I haven't tried that yet. I just tried to picture the board after the first two moves of a game."

"Oh," Danny said.

The apartment looked very nice, and there were pleasant smells coming from the kitchen. Veronica ignored the telephone message from her father on the front hall table and went to see if the chess table had arrived. It had. It was beautiful.

Veronica washed her hair and got dressed in a dark blue polished cotton dress with a pink sash.

Her mother was arranging a bowl of flowers. "Carleton sent them," she said.

"What are they?" Veronica asked. She had been hoping for red roses, the symbol of love.

"Peach blossoms," her mother said.

123

Veronica did not have to look up peach blossoms in *Flora's Dictionary*. She knew what they meant. She ran next door. "Peach blossoms!" she told Crystal.

" 'I am your captive,' " Crystal said in a matter-of-fact voice. "I suspected that's what he'd send."

Veronica went home and sat down in front of the chess table with its sixty-four pink and beige onyx squares.

She had been planning to spend the two hours before the Count arrived going through an entire game he had played against someone named Blaine using the Lowenthal Sicilian Defense.

But Veronica couldn't figure out which were supposed to be the white squares, and which were supposed to be the black. The chessmen were still in the box. Veronica looked in the box for instructions, but there were none.

There was a loud crash of thunder and a flash of lightning. The rain was beating hard against her window.

"Let me see, pink must be the same as red, and red is usually the same as white on a checkerboard, so that means beige is black, unless . . ."

At seven-fifteen the doorbell rang. Her mother wasn't ready yet, so Veronica went to answer it.

She opened the door and stood there gazing up at the international grand master.

Carleton Count was carrying an umbrella in one hand and a wet paper cup in the other. She couldn't remember the polite greeting she had rehearsed. She couldn't remember any of the grown-up conversations she had written down.

She couldn't remember anything.

"You must be Veronica," he said. "You look just like your mother."

Veronica couldn't think of anything to say.

"I'm sorry I'm a little late," he went on, "but I stopped to buy a glass of lemonade from two very nice young fellows outside the building. To my surprise they were playing chess under umbrellas. I was astounded to see they were playing the Lowenthal Sicilian Defense."

"Oh, it's quite popular around here," Veronica said shyly.

"Are they your friends?" he asked.

Veronica nodded.

He smiled at her. "May I come in?"

Veronica nodded and stood aside.

Marion appeared to take his raincoat and umbrella. Veronica noticed how gracefully he moved — never turning his back to either her or Marion.

"What a lovely apartment," Carleton Count said.

"We usually have a cat," Veronica said.

"I'm very fond of cats," Carleton said, "but I might have to take an allergy pill."

"Gulliver's not here right now," Veronica said, "but if you like I can show you some photographs of him."

"I would like that very much," Carleton said.

Veronica went to get the photographs. The conversation was not going the way she had planned, but she was very pleased that he had an interest in cats.

Veronica and the Count sat next to each other on the couch and looked at the photographs of Gulliver. Lady Jane Grey sat at the Count's feet.

Every once in a while, he reached down to pet her.

The Count asked Veronica when she had taken up chess.

"My grandfather taught me chess when I was three years old," Veronica said.

"Are you good?" the Count asked.

"I don't know," Veronica said honestly. "I only found out this week that I can see an entire chessboard in my mind. It's scary!"

"Scary?" the Count asked. "Why is it scary?"

Before she knew it, she was telling the international grand master all about it.

"I just wondered if you had ever heard of anything like that happening to any other chess players," she said.

Carleton was fascinated. "Never," he said. "Do you mean to tell me you cannot picture a chessboard without this whole scene appearing in the picture."

"*Creeping* into the picture," Veronica said, "and it gets more and more detailed." She shivered, but she no longer felt as frightened.

"Wait a minute," Carleton said. "Did you say

you played chess with your grandfather when you were three years old?"

"I know what you're thinking," Veronica said quickly, "but I'm afraid it's not his porch."

Just then Veronica's mother appeared in a soft, periwinkle-blue dress.

"Elaine!" Carleton said. To Veronica's delight, he stood up and bowed. Then he stepped forward, took her mother's hand, and raised it to his lips.

" . . . almost to his lips," Veronica told Crystal a few minutes later. She had ducked next door to bring Crystal up-to-date on the latest development. "You're not supposed to actually kiss the hand."

"Tell me something," the Count said during the soup course. "Did Veronica's grandfather really teach her chess when she was three years old?"

"Well, yes," her mother said.

"I don't remember it at all," Veronica said quickly.

Veronica was anxious to get a chance to finally hear the story. She wanted to know how they first found out she was a child prodigy at chess.

Her mother smiled. "Well, you were too young to remember. It was before your grandfather moved to Vermont — when he lived in New Hampshire."

Carleton turned to Veronica. "Did you hear that?"

Veronica was excited. "Did the house in New Hampshire have a porch and a white wicker table and a swing and . . ." Veronica described every detail.

Her mother laughed. "Veronica, you have an amazing memory!"

Carleton was smiling at her. Veronica felt very good — as if they had solved a mystery together.

"Go on," Veronica told her mother. "What happened? What happened when Grandpa taught me chess?"

"I'm not sure it's really a story for the dinner table," her mother murmured. "Your grandfather says it was a terrifying experience."

"Terrifying?" Carleton asked.

Her mother sighed. "Well, it seemed more than

likely that Veronica had eaten a pawn — a white pawn. One was missing, and she was busy chewing on another. They had to spend hours in the emergency room of the local hospital."

It *was* a startling story.

Chapter 16

Checkmate

Veronica loved watching her mother and Carleton talking together at the dinner table. Each seemed so amused by what the other was saying. They seemed to enjoy each other's company so much.

"Why don't you and Carleton play chess after we finish the salad," her mother suggested. "We can have our dessert later."

"Would you like to play?" Carleton asked her.

Veronica did not have quite as much confidence as she had had before. "I'll go set up the chess pieces," she said.

"Carleton will join you in the study in a few minutes," her mother told her.

The study? Veronica stared at her mother. Didn't she mean to say "the drawing room"?

But her mother was telling Carleton about the couple who would be renting their apartment this summer. "They were terribly pleased when they heard there was a study," she said.

"Are we renting our apartment?" Veronica asked.

"Why, yes," her mother said. "I thought I told you about it. That's why I was so anxious for you to sort through those boxes and clear out the closets."

Veronica went straight to her room and closed the door. She looked around. It wasn't her room anymore. It wasn't a drawing room, either. It was going to be a study for two people she didn't even know!

Veronica thought about Gulliver. She wanted him home very badly, but in two weeks her mother would be in the Greek islands. . . .

". . . and we'll have no place to live!"

She picked up the telephone and dialed her

father's number. It was three hours earlier there. She waited for the familiar recording: "Hey. This is Lorenzo. Down at the boatyard. Call me there."

But there was a new recording. It was a woman's voice — very prim and proper:

"You have reached the residence of Mr. and Mrs. Lorenzo Schmidt. They will be out of town until the end of August, but if you wish to reach them, you can contact them at the following number. . . ."

Veronica wrote down the number. Then she hung up. She had no intention of calling her father and his prissy new wife on their honeymoon!

Veronica was in a daze. She took the chessmen out of the box and unwrapped them. She set them on the chessboard. . . .

Then, to her horror, she saw that all the chessmen had strange carved faces. She didn't recognize any of the pieces except for the pawns because there were sixteen of them and they were the same.

"Are we ready to play?" Carleton asked.

Veronica looked up. Carleton and her mother

had come into the room. "We can't play," Veronica said.

"Why not?" her mother asked.

"There are no horses," Veronica said.

"No what?" her mother asked.

"No *horses*," Veronica said. She turned to Carleton. "You know, the ones that travel in L's."

"But it's a brand-new set." Her mother was puzzled. Carleton was looking at Veronica.

Veronica suddenly realized she had said the wrong thing.

"I mean *knights*," she said. "There are no knights."

But she had remembered too late.

Carleton examined the chess set. "It's not a standard set. I prefer the Staunton pieces myself — the ones with the horses. I'm afraid even if I show you which piece is which, you won't get used to it right away."

In the end Carleton Count and Veronica played chess on Danny's board — in black and white.

Veronica's mother invited Chris and Danny to watch the game and stay for dessert. They were very pleased with the invitation. Elaine went to help Marion get the dessert ready.

While Veronica set up the chessmen, the Count told Danny and Chris about his nephews.

"The monsters?" Veronica asked.

Carleton seemed pleased. "Oh, do you know about them? Well, Simon and Cyril had a lemonade stand that was very successful until my sister and her husband found out that they were selling the family silver at a huge discount."

Chris and Danny thought that was very funny.

When Veronica had the chessmen neatly set up, she told Carleton that if he didn't mind, she'd prefer black.

He said that was fine with him.

"And," Veronica added, "I think I should warn you, I don't take pawns."

"You don't what?" Carleton asked.

"Veronica doesn't take pawns," Danny said. "She refuses to capture them." He seemed a little embarrassed. Chris had suddenly become interested in the books along the wall.

Veronica told the international grand master a

little about her feelings of justice toward pawns and how unfairly they were treated.

"But you do know that when a pawn reaches the eighth rank — the other side side of the board — it can become a queen?" Carleton asked.

"A pawn can become a queen?" Veronica laughed. "I've never heard of such a thing."

The Count looked at her with surprise.

"Veronica," Danny said, "the pawn can become anything when it reaches the eighth rank, but usually you would choose to have the pawn become a queen."

"But a pawn is a boy," Veronica said.

Chris began talking very fast, asking the Count about a certain move he had made in the chess match the day before.

But Carleton wasn't listening.

"Let's play," he said abruptly.

Carleton Count moved the pawn in front of his king ahead two squares. Veronica did the same. The pawns were facing each other.

He moved the bishop next to his king out along the diagonal to the fourth place. Veronica copied his move exactly. Her king's bishop was now on the square in front of his.

Veronica looked up. The grand master was studying her. For the first time, she thought she saw a vicious gleam in his eye. He moved his queen along the diagonal to a square on the edge of the board on the rook's line. Veronica reached her hand forward. She stopped and pulled it back. If she moved her queen out the same way, it would be one square in front of his queen. His queen would take it!

Veronica breathed a sigh of relief. She wasn't such a bad chess player. She had seen the trap. She might even win. She looked around for a nice safe move and moved out her knight on her queen's side.

Carleton took her king's bishop's pawn with his queen. "Checkmate," he said.

"The game is over," Danny whispered.

But Veronica was studying the board. If she took his queen with her king, his bishop would take her king. . . . but her king couldn't stay where he was, the white queen would take it. . . .

"It's over," Danny said again.

But Veronica was still concentrating.

"You lost, Veronica," Chris said nervously. "It's called a fool's mate."

"Well, this one is called scholar's mate," Danny said.

"It's still a fool's mate," Chris said. "Checkmate in four moves."

There was no place for her king to move without being captured!

Tears came to Veronica's eyes. She blinked at the Count. She couldn't believe someone she liked so much could trick her so cruelly.

Elaine Schmidt came in. She was surprised the game was already over, but she announced cheerfully that dessert was being served in the dining room.

"Chess looks like fun," she said to Veronica. "You'll have to show me how to play sometime."

Chris and Danny left the room, but Carleton stayed where he was. He sat quietly across from Veronica.

Veronica sniffed back the tears. "I'm sorry I don't have any profound knowledge of the game," she whispered. "You must be awfully disappointed."

"Veronica," the grand master said, "would you like to learn chess?"

Veronica nodded. "I want to trick other people," she said. "I'm tired of other people always tricking me!"

"Is that the only reason?" he asked.

Veronica shook her head. "I love chess and I don't even know why."

"I would be honored to teach you," Carleton said.

Chapter 17

End Game

The next morning a dozen roses arrived.

They were the most beautiful roses Veronica had ever seen.

The roses were white — delicate white rosebuds.

They were the wrong color. They should have been red. White roses were not a declaration of love.

The evening had been a failure.

Her mother was disappointed. Veronica had a feeling she had been expecting red roses, too.

" 'Youth and innocence,' " Veronica read from *Flora's Dictionary*. "White means youth and innocence. That's good, isn't it? Or elegance. Elegance isn't so bad."

But it didn't help.

Her mother was quiet as she arranged them in a blue glass bowl. All at once she turned and hugged Veronica. "We did our best," she said, "and it was a lovely evening, but I'm afraid I did get my hopes up."

Veronica could not hide the roses from Crystal.

"Well, at least they're not yellow," Crystal said sadly.

It was Crystal who noticed the card. It had fallen onto the floor next to the front hall table. She picked it up.

"These roses are for Veronica!" she said. "The card says, 'Dear Veronica. Thank you for sharing your friends with me. Yours truly, Carleton Count.'"

Her mother was delighted. "I knew he liked you. Right before he left, he told me you were an enchanting child."

That doesn't sound like me, Veronica thought, but she didn't mind the idea that the Count *found* her enchanting.

A little while later, the Count called and asked if he could take them both out for lunch.

"I'm afraid I can't join you," Veronica said politely. "I have to stay home and wait for something to be delivered."

Veronica was sure her father was obeying her wishes. She was sure he was sending her cat back. She did not think his new wife sounded like the sort of person who let a cat come along on a honeymoon.

When Carleton came to pick up her mother and take her to lunch, Veronica thanked him for the roses he had sent. She checked to make sure that the roses he had just handed her mother were red (they were), and then she excused herself. "I am working on a chess problem," she told him.

When Danny came to pick up his chess set, he found Veronica playing chess against herself. She seemed to be in another world.

"Chris is telling everyone you did pretty well against Carleton Count," he said.

"But I didn't," Veronica said. "I lost in four moves."

"You could have lost even faster," Danny said.

"There's another fool's mate with checkmate in two and a half moves."

Veronica looked up from the chessboard. "Danny," she said. "Let's say you are trapped. You can't stay where you are and you have no place to move."

"Because you are in check?" Danny asked.

"No!" Veronica burst out. "Because your mother is renting your apartment, and you told your father you weren't going to Santa Barbara."

"Oh," Danny said. "I thought you were talking about chess."

Veronica was quiet. She hadn't meant to say anything.

"Does your mother know you're not going to Santa Barbara?" Danny asked.

"Not yet," Veronica said. "It's going to mess up her plans."

"Can you call your father and tell him you've changed your mind?"

"I think it's too late," Veronica said. "Although I do have a number where I can reach him."

"Call it," Danny said. "It sounds like that's your only move."

That made things easier. Veronica called the number. She got a recording.

"I'm calling my own area code," she told Danny. "They told me to hang up and dial again."

This time she got another recording: "The number you have dialed has been disconnected at the customer's request. Have a nice day."

Where had she heard that message before? She looked at the telephone number. She ran into her mother's bedroom and got the telephone book.

"What's the matter?" Danny asked.

"It's her number!" Veronica shouted. "It's Chloe Markham's number."

Danny said. "Are you all right?"

Veronica nodded. "Thanks for helping me," she said.

"Do you still want to use my chess set?" Danny asked. "I don't mind if you borrow it until you get used to the new one."

"No, thank you," Veronica said. "I have a feeling I can see this game in my head."

Danny left.

Veronica sank down into the leather armchair. She rested her elbows on the arms and put her fingertips against her temples, just the way Carleton Count did. She closed her eyes.

"Now what if," she began, "the woman who recorded the message on my father's phone is just watching the house while they're away . . .

. . . and what if Daddy and Chloe and Gulliver are on their way here right now to see me . . .

. . . and what if Daddy really does hate weddings and wanted to surprise me with the news . . .

. . . and what if . . .

Veronica opened her eyes and gasped. "That's true. He does hate weddings!"

Veronica went to find her father's letters. She opened each one and piled them on top of each other in the order they had arrived.

She never read so fast in her life:

"Let me see . . ." she muttered. "This letter says Chloe never got that job in the library in Santa Barbara. But this letter says she was offered a job in a library here." Veronica picked up the next letter in the pile. "This one says Daddy sold the boatyard. He just wants to spend his time designing boats . . ."

Veronica flipped the page and read the next

letter. "Chloe doesn't like Santa Barbara. The weather always seems to be the same, she says. They rented our house to an old lady from the Historical Society, but they can always get it back. They want to be near me. Chloe's apartment is small, but comfortable. There's plenty of room for me . . . and a baby brother or sister. . . . They both agree another child is not out of the question. . . ."

Veronica flipped to the next letter.

"They are hoping to hear from me as soon as possible. . . . They both love me. . . ."

Veronica read that line again. "We both love you . . ."

The telephone rang. Veronica picked it up.

"We just got in!" her father said.